Precipice

By

Kara Sprague

Published by Seven Mile Publishing
Scituate, Rhode Island.

Find out more about Kara Sprague at
http://www.karasprague.com

Published by Seven Mile Publishing
Scituate, Rhode Island.
http://www.sevenmilepublishing.com

Cover by Amanda Mathews at
AM Design Studios
http://amdesignstudios.net/custom-covers/

Editing provided by Lyn Worthen at
Camden Park Press
http://www.camdenparkpress.com

Precipice

By

Kara Sprague

Chapter 1

Olivia Bennett looked at her fingernails again. She had just painted them, but couldn't tell if she was satisfied with the color, a deep green, which was annoying as all get-out. It didn't even look like it had dried the same color as the swatches. She had bought the bottle on a whim, thinking it would contrast with her red hair—only it made her feel like Christmas come early.

"Ugh," Lauren grunted.

Olivia didn't have to look up to know it was Lauren. No one but Lauren could make a sound of apathetic disgust like she could. Lauren Vona was a snot at times, but Olivia adored her anyway. Lauren was almost a head taller than Olivia, with cascading dark hair and an olive complexion that gave her a seemingly perpetual tan. Olivia suspected she snuck a fake-bake in once or twice a month to keep herself darker than natural, but Olivia hadn't caught her red-handed yet. Oh, but the day she did! Lauren was going to get some serious ribbing.

Not many people could brighten Olivia's day like Lauren could; even when she was being critical, at least Lauren was honest. Olivia didn't have to worry about fake "Oh! That color looks so great with your eyes!"-shit so many other girls did to avoid hurting each other's feelings, only to let their friends walk out in public looking like clashing, over-stuffed sausages. If anything, Lauren wore her feelings a wee bit too much on her sleeve—sometimes it was like having vomit stuck to you that you couldn't wipe off.

"Do we need to send you to Dr. Henry?" Lauren asked, goading her. Dr. Henry was the ophthalmologist at Newport General Hospital, in the smallest and greatest state, Rhode Island. Tucked between Massachusetts and Connecticut, the state was affectionately known as the armpit of New England—a term made funnier by the shape of Cape Cod looking conspicuously like a flexing arm. Olivia and Lauren were both LPNs there, and previously students together at Rhode Island College, where they had met, like forever and day ago, or so it seemed.

"Ha, ha," Olivia said, but Lauren was right, she definitely needed an eye exam. All was not lost, though, the green went well with her patterned creamsicle scrubs, or at least, she thought so. "Break's over," she announced. She crushed her cigarette under foot, a disgusting habit for sure, but it was the only way to get any semblance of a break around here. The practice was going to end soon, though; the hospital was cracking down on employee's health habits. They complained about healthcare costs! A hospital complaining about the cost of healthcare. Olivia found the irony amusing.

"You going out tonight?" Lauren asked, before Olivia could slip back inside. "There's a class enrolling, ya know." Lauren said referring to the Naval Warfare Center's training program for new lieutenants. Every three months, a new class was passing through the program, training future leaders in electronic warfare. And every three months, Lauren had a new boyfriend. Olivia couldn't judge, so did she. Bright, shiny, muscular men just passing through before heading out to their assignments in need of some companionship, and Olivia and Lauren were all to happy to oblige. They had just bid their farewells to the last class, and now it was time to greet the incoming class of America's finest, in their dashing uniforms. Once, she would have been excited; now she was growing tired of the revolving door of boyfriends and the inevitable heartbreak that ensued.

"I don't know about tonight," Olivia said, trying to squirm out from bar-hopping in search of the next lieutenant.

"Come on." Lauren huffed. "If we don't go out tonight, all the handsomes will get scooped."

"Whatever. They're always available for you to steal," Olivia said.

"I know that, but thanks anyway." Lauren batted her eyes. "I'm going through withdrawal now. And I'm getting bored." Steve, her last lieutenant, had shipped out last week, apparently leaving Lauren sex-starved. They way she carried on, one would think it had been last year since she was last touched.

"You're always bored," Olivia said, trying to bait Lauren, but she shrugged it off.

"You're not still talking to Tyler are you?" Lauren looked at her, skeptically. And when Olivia didn't answer right away, alarm spread across Lauren's face. Tyler was Olivia's last Navy boyfriend. He had been in the same class with Lauren's Steve.

"We talk," Olivia admitted sheepishly, but why couldn't she still talk to him? He'd shipped out, not died. But it was against the rules. When the men shipped, that was it; it was over.

"Oh, O', you're not in love are you?" Lauren *tsked*.

"We talk on the phone. It's not like we're flying around to visit each other," Olivia said defensively. But she'd like to be. The last few months, Tyler had been endearing. They had walked the bastions of Ft. Adams, the old Civil War era fort at the entrance to Brenton Cove. With a bottle of wine and a small basket of snacks, they watched the sunset over the ramparts. An almost perfect date, if he weren't leaving the next day for San Diego.

"Long distance doesn't work. You know it, I know it, everybody knows it," Lauren said, exasperated. "Cut bait before you get hurt, hon. Come out with me tonight. You'll forget all about him."

"I can take care of myself. It's mostly him anyway, he's the needy one," Olivia said. She knew it was a little bit of a lie, but anything to deflect the conversation now. She and Lauren had burned through four different guys in the past year, and although she didn't feel like a slut or anything, she longed for a bit more . . . permanency. It didn't sound right, but as fun as things were, everything was so uncomfortably tenuous. She didn't know what she wanted, but the endless stream of cookie-cutter lieutenants wasn't it.

The intercom interrupted them, summoning them to the emergency room; all hands on deck.

"Damn," Lauren groused, smothering her cigarette.

* * *

Olivia hustled down the hall to the emergency room, Lauren a step behind her. They gloved and took up station near the doors, waiting for the emergency patient to arrive. Paramedics burst through the doors, a gurney in tow. An IV, hastily hung up on an extension arm of the gurney, swung haphazardly. An oxygen mask was secured to the patient's face. The patient swatted at the mask of the breathing bag, lethargically with a thick, rugged hand. They rolled the gurney into one of the treatment spaces and Dr. Heriberto, the on-call doctor, joined them.

"Male, early thirties, two-hundred pounds," one of the paramedics rattled off, "found in garage, suspected carbon monoxide poisoning."

Dr. Peter Heriberto barked out orders for new fluids and monitoring equipment, which Olivia and Lauren retrieved, and then turned to examining the patient's eyes. "Oxygen?"

"It's been high-flow," the paramedic said.

"Good job. We can take it from here," Dr. Heriberto said. "Olivia?"

"Yes, Doctor," Olivia piped up.

"Let's get him on our system, I don't think he's a candidate for hyperbaric treatment. Put him on a pulse oximeter and let's make sure it rises consistently for the next hour or so; then we can transfer him upstairs for monitoring. Let's get him into a johnny and make sure there are no other underlying injuries. I'll be back to check in on him in a minute." The doctor left the room.

Olivia switched the oxygen feed from the paramedic's portable bottle to the hospital's oxygen system and set it to the high flow as well. She put the plastic finger clip sensor on the man's right index finger. She couldn't help but notice his hands—large, strong, calloused and tanned, probably from outdoor work. A guy didn't get hands like those calculating spreadsheets. He was a brute of man, easily six feet tall with a developed chest and strong arms and shoulders. Quite a specimen actually. His hair was streaked with blond highlights. It was gathered in a ponytail at the back, but she thought it might hang down past his shoulders, hanging freely. His face was obscured by the mask, but from what she could see, it was as hearty and weathered as the rest of him. Definitely a man who liked the outdoors.

She wondered what color his eyes were, but didn't have time to contemplate it; the oximeter sprang to life, streaming blood oxygen level metrics, sounding an alarm and taking her out of her musing. The readout flashed a yellow 82%, but soon ticked up to 83% and then 84%. She muted the alarm. He would recover, whoever he was, provided the damage hadn't already been done. Who knew how low his oxygen level had gone prior to him being found?

Lauren grabbed a hospital gown from the supply closet and set to undressing the man.

"We're going to need some help with this slab of meat," Lauren said. "I'm not sure we can even roll him over ourselves. And if we do, I'm afraid of losing him off the other side of the bed. This guy would dent the floor if we dropped him."

Olivia quirked a smile. "We'll manage," she responded.

They set to work undressing him and going over every inch to make sure there were no other injuries. The last thing they wanted was to find out he had been stabbed or had a fractured skull or some other injury that went untreated because they hadn't looked. Olivia tried to keep focused and professional, but her eyes kept wandering over his tanned, muscled body.

"Take a look at this," Lauren said, pointing to his left leg.

A horrible scar ran from his ankle, up the outside of his shin, and inside to his calf. The skin was red and taut where scar tissue had formed. Chunks of flesh were missing, making the old injury look like a mini-canyon on the man's leg.

"How do you suppose it happened?" Olivia asked.

"Don't know, but it's totally vicious isn't it?" Lauren said, sporting a devilish smile with raised eyebrow.

They didn't find any other injury on him. Dr. Heriberto returned to the room, medical chart in hand.

"We have a name yet?" Olivia asked.

"Andrew Medina," Dr. Heriberto said.

"Medina as in the tree service?" Lauren asked, referring to Medina Landscaping & Tree Company, one of the largest tree service operators in Aquidneck Island, providing service mainly to Northeast Electric, the main operator of the electric grid in the region.

"One and the same," Dr. Heriberto responded.

The Medina family had been on the Island for generations; but being a transplant, Olivia had heard of them, but didn't know them personally. Searching her memory, she vaguely remembered the business had nearly gone under as the siblings fought for control after the patriarch's, whose name escaped her now, death. She wondered, which sibling Andrew was?

* * *

The fog clouding Andrew Medina's senses slowly, unfortunately lifted. A light was shining in his eyes, causing him to blink and he slapped at it, his arm oddly disconnected from his body.

"At least he's getting more responsive," the nitwit with the light said. "How are you feeling?"

Terrible, came to mind, but Andrew couldn't much say that to them. He pulled at the uncomfortable mask on his face. The elastic was digging into his ears. The plastic mask was small and claustrophobia-inducing. He needed to get out of here.

"Hold on, just rest." The voice was soothing. "You had an accident. Do you remember anything?"

Sure he did. What was he doing here? Who saved him?

Andrew shook his head.

"You were found on the floor of your garage with the truck running. Do you know why?"

Why had he gotten out of the truck?

He remembered Tia calling to him, but that couldn't be possible. He had seen her golden locks and cherub smile, bouncing around silly and carefree like any other four year-old would. He had gotten out of the truck to chase a ghost?

Had she saved him?

Andrew shook his head.

Things were coming into focus. The man in front of him, the doctor, wore a pleasantly neutral smile, but he knew better than to trust it; they were all butchers, just cleaner and more respected. Two women flanked the doctor, an Italian princess, not unlike Amanda—he could tell by her arrogant posture—and a redhead that could have graced the nose of a B-17 bomber. She had a pinup's hourglass figure, with curvy hips and big, round breasts. In another lifetime, he might have asked the strangely, no, *intriguingly*, anachronistic woman for her number. Now, he just felt empty and cheated. Cheated of what, he wasn't quite sure. He was supposed to be with Tia, not here, not now, but he was.

Was it a second chance? Had he sabotaged himself?

The doctor nodded and made some notes in his chart. "Have you had thoughts about harming yourself?" the doctor asked.

Andrew shook his head.

"I just remember starting up the truck, getting distracted by a phone call, and then getting all dizzy," Andrew said, his voice muffled by the oxygen mask.

The doctor nodded, but Andrew couldn't tell if he bought his fib.

"You've had carbon monoxide poisoning. We're recommending you stay here until we're sure it's flushed from your system. We have some specialists you can talk to in full confidence as well, if there is anything more you would like to discuss," the doctor said slowly, dotting over his words and delivering them like an undertaker to the deceased's family.

Andrew shook his head, and waved them away. The only thing keeping him from walking out right now was that he was unsure if his legs would carry his weight. The moment they did though, he was out of here. He didn't need word of this accident getting around town—or worse, back to his sister or to Amanda. He didn't know why he was so worried about what others thought right now. He had been on death's door of his own making. Only chance . . . or Tia . . . had brought him back for another round in this world. So he supposed it was a clarion call to reexamine his life, and salvage what he could.

"Do you have someone we can call?" The doctor asked. "Is there someone that would miss you that we can contact?"

"No," Andrew said. "I'm tired," he added, trying to derail the questioning, which surprisingly, worked. The doctor acquiesced, taking his leave, but not before reminding Andrew again that specialists were available and that he would send someone around later to see if he needed anything. Andrew assured him he would not, but he gave the doctor credit for doing his job, even if Andrew doubted his sincerity.

The nurses left, too, and Andrew found himself alone for the first time since regaining consciousness. The scar on his leg itched, but he refused to scratch it, touch it, or even acknowledge the injury existed. Through sheer will, he would banish the feeling from his body. Sometimes it threatened to drive him crazy, but he always overcame it. The itching would subside and he could resume his life again, back in control.

Chapter 2

Olivia followed Lauren out of Andrew Medina's room, both curious and a bit melancholy. Strength and defiance radiated from him, wrapped in a vulnerability she didn't quite understand but inexplicably found herself drawn to. The more she thought about it, though, the more she realized it was a sham; he was a wounded animal, scared and combative, lashing out at everyone trying to help. Dr. Heriberto had tried several times to get Andrew to open up, but that was an impossibly difficult task with such a masculine man, never mind with an audience of women looking on. Guilt nagged at her; she should have excused herself and thought of a reason to drag Lauren out of the room with her earlier. Maybe then, Andrew would have felt more comfortable talking to the doctor.

With such men, it was hard to tell, though. Being tough was such an essential part of their person, that when they were wounded they didn't know what to do. Showing weakness was not tolerated in such a man's world. Olivia had seen the same behavior in the Navy officers she and Lauren had been dating of late and, to a lesser degree, most men, in general. If she had to form a hypothesis, it might be the degree of emotional stuntedness of a man was inversely proportional to the machismo of his profession. She smiled at her own private joke, but it was a crooked smile as if she had tasted something bitter.

"You think he really tried to off himself?" Lauren asked.

After contemplating the question a moment, Olivia responded, "Yeah. I think he did."

"Why? He's loaded, handsome . . . ," Lauren said, letting her words hang, as if those were compelling enough reasons for living, and poor, ugly people should quit now.

"Who knows? Some people get stuck in a rut and can't seem to find a way out," Olivia said. "It's a vicious cycle of despair. Then death looks like a tempting way out."

"Think they'll commit him?"

"If he looks like he might try again, yeah. But I'm not sure how long Dr. Heriberto can just hold him. If he wants to do the deed, it'll be hard stopping him." Olivia said.

"Don't ever use 'do the deed' in that manner again," Lauren said giggling. "You're totally ruining my usual association for the phrase."

Olivia smiled at Lauren's gutter-mind. Andrew distracted her. She had heard of men who seemingly had everything, one day getting a pistol and blowing their brains out. Their lives devoid of meaning to the point that living seemed a chore.

But she didn't get that sense from Andrew. He seemed like a man in deep pain. Something had happened to that man that made him want to give up, which both saddened her and made her curious about him. While she had gone through some blue periods herself, they always passed; there was always something to look forward to again. Admittedly, she was going through a sort of blue period right now; a na-val-gazing period, pun intended, post-break up with Tyler—assuming she actually did cut the cord with Tyler as Lauren wanted, and stopped taking his calls and leaving his emails unanswered.

Thinking of Tyler left her fatigued. She knew that he loved her—or at least, he deluded himself with the thought that he loved her—but there was something she couldn't quite put her finger on, something that evaded her attempt to understand how he felt, or even, how she felt, that left her noncommittal and ambivalent about him. She didn't want to be flaky, but it seemed to be turning out that way. Damn the flakes.

"So are you coming?" Lauren interrupted her train of thought, but Olivia was glad for the distraction. Thinking about Tyler was bringing up all the blue feelings with partic-ular intensity just now, an intensity she blamed squarely on Andrew for some reason. Life and death situations had a way of intensifying everything around you.

"Out tonight? Of course," Olivia answered, as if the thought weaseling out of a night out hadn't been seriously occupying her mind earlier.

"Great! I knew you'd come around," Lauren said, linking her arm through Olivia's. Lauren had a way of making Oliv-ia more cheery, something she desperately needed right now. That and a mojito.

* * *

Andrew shifted uncomfortably in the hospital bed. He had been sitting there at least an hour now. The sheets were itchy, and he had couch cushions that were thicker than the mattress. A foldaway bed had a more comfortable mattress then the one he was on. It felt like every metal support in the adjustable bed was trying to monogram his backside.

His blood oxygen had returned to normal, but he had a hell of a headache. The doctor had warned him of as much. Otherwise, he was beginning to get antsy, cooped up in the small room. He had already cycled through the cable TV eight times, but there was nothing on; not that he was one to watch much television anyway.

He got out of bed, disconnecting the monitors. The boxes started to beep alarms; he scrambled clumsily to silence them. No one came running, so he assumed he was fast enough. Buzzing alarms were so common he wondered if the staff just tuned them out after a while. He looked around the Spartan room trying to figure out where they would have stuffed his clothes. A fake-wood veneer paneled cupboard caught his eye. He pulled the doors and drawers on the cheap built-in, but it was stuffed with medical supplies: towels, assorted bandages, and spare gowns. He was about to give up when he spotted one of his boots in a plastic bag. Pulling it open he found both his boots and clothes. The laces had been cut. Inspecting his clothes, they had been cut as well.

"Dammit!" They'd butchered his clothes. Except for his socks and skivvies, he had nothing to wear. Now he was going to have to get someone to bring him some clothes. All thoughts of keeping his trip to the hospital a secret disappeared. "Dammit!" He shouted again.

"Your plan to sneak away foiled?" Dr. Heriberto asked, startling him.

Andrew turned around, embarrassed at being caught.

"It's good to see you up and about, though," Dr. Heriberto said. "I came when I saw your monitor went dead. Just making sure you weren't the same."

Andrew snorted. "All you doctors have the same sense of humor, or is that just you?"

"Gallows humor makes the days bearable sometimes. And you, what keeps you sane?" the doctor asked, in a serious tone. His eyes had narrowed on Andrew, making him look for an escape. "Waiting for someone to rescue you?" The doctor asked, reading his mind.

"I can't stay here," Andrew said.

"Give me a reason to think you are well enough to leave." The doctor challenged him.

Andrew looked at him puzzled.

"Believe it or not, we do care about our patients here. Obviously you're physically well enough to checkout, but are you emotionally well enough?" Dr. Heriberto probed.

Andrew was tight lipped.

"Look, none of this leaves this room. Everything you say to me—when and why you're here, your stay here, and your checkout—is all confidential. It's protected by state and federal law. You've got nothing to fear from me," Dr. Heriberto said.

"Nothing personal, but I don't know you," Andrew said.

"That's okay. I'm not offended in the slightest. Is there someone you do trust I can send for?" Dr. Heriberto said.

Andrew shook his head.

"Are you thinking about harming yourself again?"

Andrew shook his head.

"Say it."

Andrew looked the doctor in the eye and said, "No."

"Do you mean it?"

"Yes," Andrew said, and surprisingly he meant it. He had been vacillating between suicide or not for what seemed like months. The brush with death had renewed something in him. He didn't know exactly what, only that his deliverance was some sign. It was the first shred of hope, if that's what he could call it, that he had known since Tia had died. The feeling was so alien to him that he barely recognized and still wasn't quite sure what to do with it. But it was a handhold that he could grip onto, no matter the pain that he didn't dare let go.

"Good. Why?" The doctor asked.

"What?"

"Why won't you go try again?"

"I just won't," Andrew said. "I can't explain it. I just know I won't."

The doctor studied him for a short while, like he was trying to divine Andrew's soul. Andrew couldn't tell if he was reflecting on their conversation or trying to decide whether he could believe him. There was no reason why he should, and if their positions were reversed, Andrew would probably have put himself on the short bus to Butler, the loony bin in Providence.

"I think I believe you, but protocol requires we hold you until we're sure that you aren't going to have another accident the moment you walk through those doors," Dr. Heriberto said, pointing to the exit. Andrew couldn't resist looking; he wanted to get out of the hospital so bad. "Liability, you understand. We don't want to get sued by your next of kin."

"That won't be an issue," Andrew said.

"Because . . . ," Dr. Heriberto prompted.

"I'm alone."

"You'd be surprised at who comes out of the woodwork at the scent of money." The doctor, smiled weakly. "But let's examine that thought. What makes you think you are alone?"

* * *

Olivia sidestepped the gurney blocking her way, and into the nurse's station in the main ward. She perused the monitors briefly for anything out of whack before looking at the scheduled rounds. With relief, she saw that the rest of the shift was light. She had agreed to cover the first half of Kate Baum's shift so she could see her kid's recital; hopefully there would be no more drama and she could leave by nine. Lauren had already gone and was likely catching a nap before the evening's hunt. A small pang of regret gnawed at her for agreeing to go, but she knew she needed to get herself back out there and her mind off of Tyler—and nothing cleared the mind of regret like a night of heavy drinking and debauchery; the regret could wait until the next morning.

She tidied up the counter, loaded her cart and started the rounds. Her mind kept drifting back to Tyler. He had arrived safely in San Diego, where he was stationed at Coronado doing something or other; she couldn't remember what, the jargon escaped her. It was kind of shameful she couldn't remember, considering he had painstakingly explained it to her not too long ago, but she tried not to take it to heart too much. Tyler probably only remembered her as a nurse anyway, just like she remembered him as a sailor. Generic terms that summoned meaning, but only conveyed a romanticized image of the job. He was likely pushing paper, like she did nowadays with insurance carriers and Medicaid, or pushing pixels, rather, with the new computerized systems.

Still, their last conversation bothered her. She hadn't mentioned it to Lauren yet, because, well, Lauren was Lauren—scratch one lieutenant, onto the next—but Tyler had nearly convinced her to quit and move to San Diego with him. The thought of moving west and leaving everything behind was both tempting and terrifying. A new beginning, but her identity defined by belonging to Tyler. Not that belonging to someone didn't have its appeal, but she was kind of attached to her identity and it frightened her that his might subsume hers. She had heard of the Officer's Wives Club, with its real housewives and drama. She had also seen the darker side of being a Navy wife, the loneliness and resulting temptation that brought them to the Newport bars while their husbands were at sea. She didn't think she could stand that.

She also would have to get licensed in California, an idea Tyler pooh-poohed, arguing that she wouldn't need to work, if she lived on base with him. That stuck in her craw. She had put herself through nursing school and supported herself. The idea of giving up her career to become a stay-at-home wife kind of pissed her off, but she could see the appeal. Even Lauren had the not-so-unstated goal of becoming a housewife.

Olivia had just finished up her rounds when she thought she heard someone calling her name.

"Olivia," Dr. Heriberto called to her, his head poking out of one of the patient rooms.

She stopped pushing her cart and walked over to him.

"Come in. I have a favor to ask," he said, holding the door open for her.

She entered the room and was surprised to see it occupied already. Andrew was seated in a chair in nothing but a gown. He glanced up at her; his deep brown eyes boring a hole in her, making her catch her breath. She recomposed herself quickly, but he quirked a smile at her. She couldn't help but blush, making her feel all the more frazzled. *Was this man playing with her?*

"Thanks for coming in," Dr. Heriberto said. "Andrew is going to stay with us for the night, maybe another, but he needs some of his stuff."

"Yeah?" Olivia said blankly, wondering where she fit into this equation.

"We were wondering if you could make a quick trip to his house and grab some things for him?"

"What?" Olivia said incredulously. The request was highly unusual. Didn't Andrew have any family?

Andrew spoke up now, drawing her attention to him and his smoldering eyes. Afraid she would blush again, she focused on his mouth, which was a huge mistake. His lips were even more hypnotizing than his eyes. She wondered what they tasted like, what it would feel like to have them working their way down her body.

"I just need a few things," Andrew said, snapping her out of her stupor, "Because my clothes . . . , well, they didn't survive." He pointed at a clear bag on the windowsill containing the remnants of his clothing.

"Andrew needs some discretion right now," Dr. Heriberto said. "He can't call people he knows."

"I think I understand," Olivia said, piecing things together. *Andrew didn't want people to know he had been to the hospital.* "When should I go?"

"Now," Dr. Heriberto said.

Olivia looked at him, starting to protest.

"Don't worry about the rest of your shift," Dr. Heriberto said. "I'll get someone from one of the other floors to cover it. They're overstaffed on fourth floor anyway. You can cut out early tonight."

Olivia nodded. Looking over at Andrew, she said, "How do I get to your place?"

"Thank you," Andrew said, flashing her a smile. "I appreciate it more than you know."

Chapter 3

Olivia swung by the apartment that she shared with Lauren first. She stripped down from her scrubs and slipped into black pants and a backless, emerald shirt. The pants were fitted at the top and swishy at the bottom, great for dancing and showing off her ass. The emerald shirt was one of her favorites, too—an oversized bib really, as it showed a tantalizing amount of side-boob. She grabbed a pair of black kitten-heeled sandals to round out the outfit. Together, the combination would attract attention of the sort she and Lauren were after tonight.

She found Lauren soaking in the tub, nearly pruned.

"Have you been in there since you punched out?" Olivia asked, enviously, trying to disguise it with a disapproving tone. Olivia set to work, reconstituting her hair and makeup for the night's hunt.

"Nearly." Lauren said, and stuck her tongue out at Olivia. "What time is it?"

"Seven."

"You're back early," Lauren said. Once Lauren got a look at Olivia's outfit, she added, "And va-va-voom, you're pulling out the stops. That's my girl! Hand me a towel?" Olivia grabbed a towel and handed it to Lauren.

"Heriberto let me go early if I ran him an errand," Olivia said.

"Coffee again?" Lauren asked referring to the time Dr. Heriberto had bribed them to go on a Dunkin run for him. Lauren got up from the tub, wrapping herself in the towel.

"Nah, I'm fetching some clothes for Andrew Medina." Lauren looked at her blank-faced. "The patient we admitted today," Olivia added.

"Oh, the hottie woodcutter," Lauren said, smiling devilishly.

"That's the one," Olivia confirmed, sporting a wry smile of her own.

Olivia gave her teeth a quick brush and refreshed her deodorant before standing back to examine the results. To top things off, she gave her neck and cleavage a squirt of perfume. Tonight she would cure herself of any feelings for Tyler.

"You're a goddess. Don't be late," Lauren said. "The bars will start filling up soon."

"I won't" Olivia said, begging off to do the clothing run. "Meet you back here?"

"Nah, I'll be at Orchid, maybe the Parrot, warming the boys up for your arrival," Lauren said, referring to two of the haunts and watering holes where the lieutenants usually congregated. Their usual route was along America's Cup Avenue and Thames Street, hitting the different hole-in-the-wall bars, before turning back up Trouro Street on their way back to their apartment in downtown Newport. It was a cra-

zy pub-crawl—or trawl in their case—that had been spectac-
ularly successful in snagging lieutenants.

Their only real competition were the coeds from Salve
Regina and Roger Williams University who often came
downtown for some wild fun; but now that summer was
here, most of the student body had returned home, leaving
locals, which were ill-equipped for the double-sexpot-blast
of Lauren and Olivia. Or so they amusingly liked to think.

"Okay, I'll see you there," Olivia said, grabbing a black
clutch and tucking her license and some cash into it. She
snagged her keys and descended the narrow staircase to the
street below where she had left her late-model Miata, with
its sun-bleached red paint, parked on the street. She got in
the car and pulled out the key Andrew had given her with
the slip of paper rubber-banded around it and read his address for the first time. Indian Avenue leapt out at her. She
gave a low whistle. Waterfront property.

She cut over to Memorial Boulevard, over Easton Beach,
and onto Purgatory Road. As she passed the beach, the scent
of the heavy salty air triggered a sense of nostalgia and a bit
of excitement at the impending summer. The Easton and
Second beaches had always been her summer hangouts, and
she looked forward to soaking in the rays this summer with
Lauren, and a never-ending stream of fruity drinks from the
Beach Club.

Purgatory Road turned into Paradise Road, which she
didn't stay on long before bearing right onto Hanging Rock

Road, and away from Second Beach. She hadn't been over this way on the island in a long time, and had never really had occasion to drive up Indian, where mansions overlooked the ocean cliffs at the Atlantic.

She watched the house numbers creep slowly towards Andrew's until she finally reached his driveway. There was no gate, like the other estates surrounding it. In fact, the house at the end of the drive was conspicuously small—much smaller than some of the surrounding estates, but it blended with the landscape better and seemed sized to fit its lot, rather than occupying every square inch of the terrain like its larger neighbors. Maybe Medina wasn't as rich as Lauren had thought? Looking past the house, an impressive view of the Atlantic Ocean and Little Compton, across the bay, stretched out in front of her. And, by golly, it looked like a vineyard was growing on the ground sloping to the ocean.

One of the garage doors was open, revealing the tailgate of a big Chevy truck with dualie tires, reminding her of how she'd met Medina. Had he attempted suicide in that garage?

Avoiding the garage for now, she parked her car near the front door. She let herself into the ornate foyer, and let out a low whistle. A floor medallion was centered under a chandelier, and wainscoting decorated the walls, which were also festooned with picture rails and built-up crown molding, painted a creamy white offset by the flat, dark grey of the wall. A winding staircase with wrought-iron banister led upstairs, but Andrew had said his bedroom was on the ground floor, near the rear of the house, adjoining the kitchen.

She walked down a short hall and into the next room. Obviously the entertainment room, it was dominated by a large, dust-coated, flat-screen television, couches, and chairs. An ornate fireplace occupied the other wall. At least he hadn't hung the television above the fireplace as if it were an oil painting, like so many did nowadays. She continued to the next room and found a large table and chairs, which seemed to have been converted to a makeshift office, with piles of papers covering every square inch of the table, and piles of folders stacked in the chairs and against the walls.

The next room—a breakfast room—was a wall of windows, overlooking a deck and displaying the stupendous view she had glimpsed from the driveway. Her breath caught as she took it all in. The kitchen was off to her left.

The kitchen was shockingly tidy, she wondered if he used it at all, which was disappointing to see such a glamorous kitchen go to waste.

She spotted a door leading out of the kitchen, which she presumed was Andrew's bedroom, as he had told her it adjoined the kitchen. Leaving the kitchen behind, she entered his bedroom. The bedroom was as messy as she would have expected any man's bedroom to be, strewn with clothes, the frameless bed unmade. A chandelier hung in the room, making her think the room had been converted from other purposes. A pair of French doors led to the deck, revealing the spectacular bay view, making her catch her breath again.

Turning her attention back to the task at hand, she found a small duffle and grabbed a couple pairs of jeans, the only pants that seemed available, and a couple of pocketed t-shirts emblazoned with the Medina logo. She found a pair of tennis shoes next to the dresser and stuffed those in as well, remembering how they had snipped the laces on his boots. White tube socks followed the shoes into the bag. His underwear, mixed in the same drawer with the loose socks, weren't tighty-whities, bringing a wry smile to her face. She glossed over the boxers, the briefs catching her attention. These puppies were Calvin briefs, with nary a bit of elastic holding the front to the back. She held them up imagining Andrew filling them out.

"Who the fuck are you?" A woman's voice in a grating pitch sent a shiver down Olivia's back.

Olivia's first instinct was to turn and start sputtering inanities, but the woman's bitchy tone somehow enabled her to keep it together. Not turning, Olivia looked over her shoulder at the woman, trying to project unconcern and confidence, even though her guts were roiling. She knew she'd pulled it off when the woman stiffened with barely-concealed rage.

The woman had long, cascading black hair, so black Olivia swore it had a cobalt sheen to it. She was tall and thin, with a pair of obviously fake boobs, and was about

Olivia's age, maybe a year or two older. She wore a pink velour tracksuit and three-inch platforms. A chintzy, pink metallic bag was slung over her shoulder. She had keys and a Frappuccino in one hand and a pair of Jackie-O sized sunglasses in the other. *Gotta love that Italian style.*

Was this trash Andrew's girlfriend?

Olivia was suddenly conscious of how she was dressed and how this woman might take her presence here. She tasted a tang of guilt, but at the same time found something incredibly grating about the woman and decided she couldn't let her off the hook quite yet. She knew it was mean to trick this woman, but she was feeling mischievous.

The woman recovered from her moment of rage and repeated, "What are you doing here?"

Olivia turned to face her slowly, adding a touch of sensuality to it, making sure the woman got a good view of her.

"I just came to grab Andrew some clothes," she said innocently, holding up Andrew's Calvin's, which of course, had the desired effect, sending the woman into a boiling rage.

"Andrew and I go way back. He may think he's taking a hiatus, but he'll back sooner or later, hon, and you'll be nothing but a vague memory." The woman said, slashing with her hand to emphasize her words.

So this was Andrew's *ex*. He couldn't have possibly wanted to off himself over this piece of trash, could he?

"I think there's only one vague memory standing in this room now," Olivia snapped back. Why she was getting territorial with this woman she couldn't quite figure. She didn't want to make Andrew's life any more difficult than it already obviously was, but she'd also decided that whoever this woman was and whatever relationship she had had with Andrew, he'd decided to end it some time ago; Olivia was just adding some finality to that decision. And, admittedly, she was having a lot of fun at this woman's expense.

"You know nothing. Andrew and I are connected," she said, tapping her pinched fingers together, "and nothing is ever going to take that away, including some redheaded slut." A tear rolled down the woman's face, which she angrily brushed away.

Olivia began to think maybe she had gone too far in injecting herself into Andrew's private life, but it was a bit too late to have regrets now. Plus, the woman's nasty disposition made it too easy. The incongruity wasn't lost on Olivia that she likely would have been a little bit more than irate herself at finding another woman going through the underwear in her boyfriend's bedroom.

"That connection died, hon," Olivia said, mustering as much bravado and flippancy as she could in the retort.

The woman's demeanor shrunk like Olivia had suckerpunched her. Her lip trembled and a choked back cry escaped.

"You're a cunt," the woman said, between gibbers. Without another word and before Olivia could retort, the woman turned and left, hurrying away from Olivia.

Olivia let out the breath she hadn't realized she had been holding. She finished packing Andrew's bag. Tires screeched as Olivia heard a car peel out of the driveway. She hoped the bitch hadn't keyed her car. She knew it was unlikely, but some people never outgrew high school, like the girls that still wore velour tracksuits and thought it was stylish.

Satisfied she'd gotten everything Andrew had asked for, she turned her attention to the garage, the last place he thought his smartphone would be. She locked the house back up and ventured over to the open garage. In addition to the truck, a speedboat in a trailer occupied the middle bay, and dolled up Chevelle in the third. Andrew really was a Chevy guy.

She walked over to the truck—it was open, the door hanging ajar—and looked in. It looked like a mobile office, with papers and empty coffee cups and pens strewn about the passenger seat and floor. She checked the dash, but didn't find the phone. She closed the cab door and was about to leave when a glint caught her eye near the wheel well. Stooping down, she found the phone lying within crushing distance of the tire. Olivia smiled at her discovery.

She picked up the phone. It was scuffed from use, but didn't appear damaged. The screen was intact. She thumbed one of the buttons, and the screen lit up. There were a bajillion missed calls, likely a bunch from the bitch she met earlier and one outgoing call . . . to 911. Apparently Andrew'd had a change of conscience. She wondered again what had brought that man, who seemingly had everything—or at least a hell of a lot more than everyone else—to nearly take his life.

She dusted off her pants. Before she left, started the garage door down. She scooted under it quickly, before it closed, and walked to her car.

"Motherfucker," Olivia exhaled.

In the driver's seat, an empty plastic cup sat in pool of melting Frappuccino.

Chapter 4

Andrew had given up on trying to find anything on the limited cable channels on the hospital television, and stood by the locked window, looking out at the city lights. He didn't watch television . . . normally.

But that was the rub; nothing was normal about his situation now, or at least that hadn't been brewing for a while. The doctor had given him a lot to think about. He was still too confused to make sense of it. He didn't exactly feel like he'd turned a corner or anything, just that the world seemed a little less painful than it had been hours ago, a little more bearable.

He wanted to start to piece things together of the shattered remains of his life. He didn't quite know where to start other than to throw himself back into work. At least there, he could be productive again. Of course, that would mean damage control. He'd been neglecting things at the office for weeks now. The problem focused his attention, drawing it away from everything else that threatened his grip on today. *One step, inch-by-inch, find a reason to go on. Don't look too far ahead, because overwhelming despair might creep back in.*

He glanced at the card the doctor had left him for the Samaritans, a suicide prevention non-profit. He didn't know if he could get his head around talking to strangers about anything so personal. He'd promised the doctor he would give them a call, and he didn't make such promises lightly.

But it was a new concept for him—letting people in to see his scarred innards.

A soft knock at the door grabbed his attention.

The redheaded nurse, Olivia, came in, wiping away all thoughts of anything but her. He had thought she was attractive earlier, but now, she totally blew him away. Her shirt—if it could be called that—barely covered her creamy skin, revealing flashes of her navel and the curvature of her generous breasts. Her arms were toned. She walked quickly towards him, her hips swaying hypnotically. The black pants she wore, hugged her thighs and waist, revealing the gap between. Her painted toes peeked out from the cuff of her pant legs as they seductively swirled, suggesting the shape of her calves. She was captivating.

Andrew looked back up to her face. Her brow was furrowed, mouth drawn thin, framed in jouncing red curls making the visage the sexiest anger he had seen. Why she was angry, he hadn't a clue, but he wanted to thank whoever had crossed her.

When their eyes connected, her anger diffused and her breath caught. She looked away quickly, cheeks flushing. Was she embarrassed—or did she find him attractive?

Looking back at him after she had a chance to recompose herself, she said, "Success. You got a change of clothes and I found your phone in the garage." Olivia extended the bag to him.

He reached for the bag, his fingertips brushing against her hand as he took possession of the bag, sending an electric thrill through him; one he noticed was shared by her reaction to his touch. Olivia pulled her hand hastily away from the bag, but her blush betrayed her feelings.

"Thank you," Andrew said.

He stepped closer to her, moving inside her personal space. The aggressive move startled her, but she didn't back away. She looked up, lips parted, trembling to form words. He didn't give her a chance to speak. Leaning in, he kissed her on the lips. She received the kiss tentatively at first, yielding to him. But soon was giving as good as she received, attacking his kiss with gusto. Their lips danced together, tongues darting into one another's mouths and tangling.

His arm slid around her waist and up her bare back, pulling her close. Her arms moved around his shoulders in response. He felt her breasts press against him, her nipples hard through her ridiculous shirt. He parted their kiss and worked his way down her chin and neck. Olivia let out small sighs and gasps as he nibbled at her salty flesh.

He lowered a hand to her ass, grabbing a cheek full in his hand. He lowered his other hand to her ass and picked her up, turned, then dropped her on the hospital bed. She grunted with the impact, her legs dangling off the side.

"This is crazy," Olivia said, gasping.

Andrew moved between her legs and leaned down over her, kissing her before she could speak again. His right hand slid between her legs, rubbing her mound. She let out another gasp as he worked her button. She moaned uncontrollably. He propped himself above her on his right forearm and continued to devour her neck, chin, and mouth, wandering freely between them.

"I could get fired. Lose my license," Olivia breathed, but they sounded like she was trying to persuade herself to stop, not asking him.

He straightened up and slid his hands to her hips. Grabbing her pants, he pulled them down to her knees. She wasn't wearing any panties and her bush was red, neat and trimmed. He lifted her legs up. Holding them together, he pushed her knees vertical, perpendicular with her pelvis, revealing her to him.

He probed her gently with a finger, exploring inside her. Olivia trembled and gasped with each flick of his finger. She was his completely to control.

Her rolled her over, face down. She let out a whimper. Pulling the ties at his shoulder and waist, the johnnie fell away from him. He shoved his underwear down and kicked it the rest of the way off, not able to get rid of them fast enough. Twisting, Olivia looked back at him as he prepared to enter her. She lifted her hips to him in anticipation, as her eyes roved his body, ultimately focusing on his erect cock.

She inhaled as he rubbed the tip against the lips of her pussy, soaking it in her juices. She made a frustrated noise at his teasing. He pushed into her, just the tip, and pulled back out again. Repeating the motion, much to Olivia's frustration. He pushed the tip in again, this time she shoved backwards, taking him entirely into her. Groans escaped both of them, as he slid deep into her slick passage.

"Fuck me now," Olivia commanded.

* * *

Olivia's body was trembling uncontrollably in an anticipation of Andrew's ministrations. With her pants restraining her ankles, her mobility was frustratingly limited. She was at his mercy, which she found both unnerving and deeply thrilling. He had manhandled her up to now, but she needed him to finish the job. Her thighs were slick with her juices and her pussy ached for him to be inside her. She could tell he wanted to also, but he was deliberately teasing her.

And then she realized, whether he knew it or not, it was as if by controlling her, dominating her, he was reasserting his control in the world—a world that had seemingly spun out of control for him not too long ago. The chaos of whatever had been occurring in his life had been overwhelming. But here, now, she could change that for him. She would help him heal and regain that confidence to live again.

"Please," she pleaded, when he didn't jump to her barked command. "I need you in me," she added, in as submissive a voice as she dared. She reached back with a hand and grabbed her right ass cheek, spreading herself for him. She swayed her hips and sighed.

Her actions had the desired effect. He grabbed her wrist firmly and pulled her hand out of his way.

Releasing her arm, he aligned himself with her. She watched with eager anticipation, licking her lips. He thrust into her suddenly, making her yelp with its forcefulness. Not that he hurt her, but more out of surprise at his ferociousness. He thrust into her vigorously, barely giving her a chance to catch breaths between each surge of pleasure as the head of his cock relentlessly stroked against her g-spot. She moaned and gasped, balling the bed sheets in her fists as she fought to maintain some semblance of control over her body. Her knees were shaking and buckling and she doubted she could have held herself up save for Andrew's iron grip on her hips.

The room echoed with her moans and the rhythmic slap of Andrew's strokes in her. She prayed no one heard, but couldn't imagine stopping for anything now. She needed him, and he, her.

Olivia trembled and her knees buckled again. She held her breath as the spring inside her coiled tightly. She couldn't hold it any longer. The spring releasing, her orgasm burst through her body and she clenched forcefully around Andrew. He let out a gasp, letting her know he had felt her come. She felt herself clench repeatedly as the shockwaves of the orgasm past through her like the aftershocks of an earthquake.

Andrew hadn't slowed a bit, continuing to fuck her relentlessly. The stimulation turned to overstimulation. Her loins quivered with each stroke, the line blurring between pleasure and pain.

"I'm not sure I can take anymore," Olivia pleaded.

She was face-first in the sheets, panting in time with each of Andrew's strokes.

"Relax. Roll with it. We're almost there," Andrew reassured her. "There's another one in you."

Olivia snorted, but tried to comply. She slowed her breath, and let herself go limp in Andrew's hands. She focused on Andrew's cock sliding in and out of her pussy. Andrew thrust deeper and longer into her, slowing his stroke. Abruptly, the overstimulation that was almost painfully overwhelming moments ago evolved into a ball of radiating pleasure, engulfing her core. She hadn't experienced anything like it before.

"What are you doing to me?" She gasped.

"Hold on a bit more," Andrew said.

She was mystified by his endurance, but couldn't dwell on it as the radiating ball in her core grew and grew. She sucked in a breath and writhed, uncontrollably on the bed as the pleasure built and built inside of her. *Who was this man and where had he been all her life?*

"Relax," Andrew said gently. "Let the wave wash over you."

She stilled her body and exhaled as he'd instructed, trusting him with her body, trusting she would reach new peaks of ecstasy, which seemed rapidly approaching. Andrew kept the deliberate pace, which was riding between the cusp of pleasure and pain.

"Oh, god!" She panted, feeling herself cresting.

"Don't chase it. Let it come to you, baby," Andrew said, huskily.

And the orgasm broke over her like Andrew said it would. The ball of pleasure that had been building and building broke free of its confines traveling up her spine and down to her toes, touching every part of her. Her breaths drew raggedly as the ripples of the orgasm lapped across her.

Andrew's steady strokes in her stuttered and he grunted. He was coming, too. She looked back at him languidly, seeing his face caught in the rictus of orgasm. He huffed and steadied himself, drawing himself from her.

She felt relieved to have the source of the nearly unbearable stimulation removed—and a pang of emptiness.

She rolled to her side and Andrew collapsed across the bed next to her. She leaned over and kissed him slowly, gently pulling at his lower lip. He kissed her nose and lay back, sighing.

She sat up and pulled her pants back up over her knees, then stood and shuffled over to one of the cabinets. Rummaging around, she found a cloth.

Feeling eyes on her, she looked up to see Andrew surveying her.

"Don't look," she said. Why she felt embarrassed at cleaning herself in front of him, she couldn't put a finger on, but he obeyed, looking away from her with a grin.

She cleaned the sex off of her and hiked her pants back up to their proper place. Based on how tender she felt now, tomorrow was going to be uncomfortable. She straightened her shirt and stole quickly into his bathroom to check her makeup, which was surprisingly intact; except for her lipstick, which had been obliterated by their frenetic kissing.

"Thank you," Andrew said.

She saw he had sat up and was looking at her again. She smiled weakly at him, feeling very self-conscious.

What had she been thinking?

Andrew was a complete stranger to her and a patient. She was a nurse here. This was completely inappropriate no matter how amazingly good the sex was . . . no matter how sexy he looked . . . how strong his shoulders and hands were . . . no matter how amazing his cock had felt in her—she needed to stop this train of thought right now.

Stepping out of the bathroom, she looked around for her clutch and keys. She needed to remove herself from the room before she decided to stay with him.

Andrew watched her, making her a little crazy. She nearly knocked an IV stand over, and stubbed her toe on the caster of a crash cart, making her wince painfully.

"Help you find something?" He asked, puzzled.

She childishly ignored him as if it somehow made her actions disappear if she pretended he didn't exist. Where were her keys and clutch? She stooped and looked under the bed, but there was no "under the bed" as it was filled with the lift mechanism.

A jeaned pant leg moved in her view. Looking up, it was Andrew. He had gotten his pants on anyway. He was barefoot and bare-chested, making her feel a little weak in the knees, making her want to unzip him and see how much stamina he really had. She shook her head, trying to jar the thought loose.

"Looking for these?" He held her keys and clutch.

She jumped up smiling and extended a hand for them.

"Not so fast," he said, pulling them away from her outstretched hand.

"I have to go," Olivia snapped, harsher than she would have liked. She regretted her tone immediately.

His face grew stony and he handed her the items. Now she felt a bit guilty, but she needed to get out of here, needed to collect her thoughts.

"I'm sorry," she said.

"You'd better get going before someone comes to check in on me," he said, letting her off the hook.

Now she really felt guilty and confused. She didn't want him to protect her. She should have been protecting him.

Instead she had taken advantage of his vulnerability with her authority.

She nodded regretfully at him and turned to escape.

He grabbed her hand, stalling her departure. Tugging on her fingertips, he gave her a reassuring smile. She didn't feel reassured, though. She pulled her hand free and hurried out of his room.

Chapter 5

Olivia pressed through the bodies crowding the Black Orchid. A hand—she thought was a hand anyway—dragged a little too slow across her backside; a hazard and (if random, anonymous, copped-feels swung your way) benefit, of the clubs. She almost turned and punched the nearest person, but she couldn't be bothered with it now. Lauren was a bit irate with her, she noted by the five or so texts asking where the hell she was. Apparently she had scored and needed her wingman urgently.

Since "getting cleaved by the woodcutter's axe" wasn't an acceptable answer, Olivia had ironically responded, "coming" instead. It wasn't her first one-night-stand, and certainly not the first time she had regretted having sex with a guy, but Andrew had certainly been the most reckless sex she had ever had . . . and the most splendidly intense.

She looked back down at her phone in her hand as it buzzed, indicating a message received.

here yet? at the back.

Lauren's impatience was getting irritating. She needed a drink.

Clusters of Navy men in their dress whites populated the bar, mixing in with the locals. Joel, the bartender, gave Olivia a salute with his bottle opener before opening six ponies he had arranged in a bucket of ice. The combination of his goatee, receding salt-and-pepper mullet, and Hawaiian shirt always made Lauren and her giggle. He had arms like cannons that looked even more ridiculous whenever he came out from behind the bar and she saw his stick-legs poking out from a pair of knee-length shorts. She flashed him a smile and continued to press to her destination, which apparently was a table near the back.

Finally able to see past the crush, Olivia found Lauren, perched, not-so-demurely, on a beefy lieutenant's lap. His hat was askew and collar undone. The rest of the table was surrounded with four other lieutenants. Four buckets of ponies were in the middle of the table; they must have been on sale, Olivia thought. She got more than a look-over from the guys at the table—exactly the reaction her outfit was designed to elicit—but she was feeling more than a bit shy now and wished she had chosen something a little less revealing. Of course, something a little less revealing might have deprived her of her encounter with Andrew, too, which still wheedled at the back of her mind.

Stupid, stupid.

"Hey!" Lauren squealed. She hopped off of Lieutenant Beef's lap and they embraced. Lauren even gave her a couple of pecks on the cheek, giving Olivia a good whiff of her breath; Lauren was well on her way to being drunk.

Olivia put on a fake smile and hugged Lauren back. Detecting something amiss, Lauren gave her a curious look.

"I'm okay," Olivia said, trying to deflect further questioning until later.

Lauren's eyes narrowed, but she moved on, introducing everyone around the table; Olivia promptly forgot their names, if she had heard them in the first place.

Man, she was really off of her game right now.

The men made room for her and she sandwiched herself at the table between two of them. One of them, Jeremy, she thought, offered her a beer, which she accepted. Lauren blathered on, making some joke—or what she thought was a joke—and everyone laughed. Olivia chuckled too, in Pavlovian fashion, to avoid standing out, but her laugh sounded fake even to her.

She really wanted to go home right now and end the night, but she had promised Lauren. Plus, she still wasn't sure if she wanted to be alone, where her thoughts might dwell on Andrew. At least here she had a hope of obliterating the memory of the carnal encounter, that is, if she could ground herself present. Detached as she was, it was hard to focus on anything but Andrew and the pleasant and confused feelings still coursing through her body.

"Huh?" Olivia said.

The lieutenant that had given her the beer was speaking to her, but she hadn't registered a word he had said. Dark brown hair framed his baby blue eyes, which would have normally got her motor running.

"You're pretty distracted," he said, smiling down at her.

She blushed and looked at her beer. Looking back up at him she said, "Sorry. I'm so embarrassed. My mind is elsewhere, Jeremy."

"Justin," he corrected.

Now she felt doubly embarrassed.

"Don't worry about it," he said, reassuringly. "I'm not offended. We just met." He smiled, then took another swig from his beer. "Your friend is kind of wild," Justin said, indicating Lauren.

"She has her moments," Olivia said. "She wasn't dancing on the tables earlier, was she?"

Justin laughed and said, "No."

"Great. I arrived in the nick of time," Olivia said, snapping her fingers.

"Somehow I doubt you're her chaperone"

Olivia made a face of faux offense. "What does that mean?"

"I think you're probably wilder than she is." Justin gave her a knowing smile.

He didn't know the half of it, but she didn't like where this conversation was going—and it was hitting a little too close to home. It was one thing for *her* to think she was being a little on the slutty side, maybe okay for Lauren to point it out, but a complete stranger? No, Justin was stepping out of bounds.

She shifted her attention back to Lauren, who wasn't in any position to talk—Lauren was completely caught up looking into Beef's eyes. Maybe she could excuse herself?

"I've offended you"

Justin, again.

She looked back at him out of the corner of her eyes, letting her annoyance show.

"I'm sorry, I didn't mean to."

He gave her a puppy dog look that made her laugh.

"It's okay. I'm a bit distracted and feeling prickly," Olivia said.

"What do you do?"

"Nurse. We're both nurses," Olivia said, pointing her beer at Lauren.

"Tough job." It was a statement, not a question.

But it had its benefits, like fucking your nut-job patients.

Her thoughts must have expressed themselves strangely on her face.

"Are you bored?"

"No, just tired and . . ."

"Distracted," Justin finished.

Olivia looked at him with narrowed eyes. She couldn't decide whether he was inherently annoying or she was just being overly sensitive.

"Wanna get some air?" Justin suggested, pointing at the patio. Air was tempting, but she didn't want to leave Lauren.

"Come on," he said standing up.

He pulled on her upper arm, and she relented, standing with him. The booth was cramped and Lauren wasn't going anywhere, she convinced herself, even though, she had no interest in flirting with Justin or anyone else tonight. She certainly wasn't hooking up—she had already checked that box. Or rather Andrew had checked *her* box . . . thoroughly . . . completely.

She shook her head in an attempt to bring herself back to now.

She followed Justin to the patio. The cool night air brought goose pimples to her arms, but the chill was preferable to the stuffiness of the bar. The music was vibrated her bones. The DJ was working the turntables, sending an infectious bass through her spine. People were gyrating to the beat on open-air dance floor.

Justin moved onto the dance floor. Ditching her beer on a windowsill, Olivia followed him into the melee. She let her hips sway and head shake. Holding her arms above her head, she twisted and jerked to the pulsing beat. Justin was there, just behind her. She felt his presence in her personal space, but he didn't touch her.

Dancing was what she needed; it blasted her mind clear, like dynamiting a channel through a chasm. There were no worries, no future, no consequences, no obligations, only now.

He placed a hand on her hip, and she slid out from under it. She twirled in front of him teasing; he could get close, watch her, but not touch. She turned her side to him, undulating her body. She could see it had the desired effect. His eyes were riveted on her, his face expressionless, desire simmering under his skin. The tempo increased and so did Olivia's gyrations.

He placed his hand on her hip again. Again, she stepped back and away from his fingertips. She smiled coyly and kept her distance. He didn't smile at her playfulness, though. Apparently, he didn't care for teases. No, not one bit. That was too bad, because now he definitely was going to end up frustrated tonight. If there was one thing that annoyed Olivia about the barhopping scene it was the sense of entitlement some of the guys seemed to get if she showed a little interest. Maybe she was being a bit unfair to him, but she didn't want to be groped right now—and Justin had the groping look about him.

Olivia twirled and smile at him playfully again, which probably wasn't the nicest thing to do, but she was still out of sorts.

Justin timed his move, and stepped into her mid-twirl. She grabbed onto him to stop from falling over. He wrapped her up in his arms, and didn't miss a dance beat. Olivia might have been impressed with the grace of the move if she weren't stewing now. She felt his soft, warm hands on her skin, completely opposite of Andrew's rough, weathered mitts.

Justin smiled at her, but all she wanted to do was punch the smug look off his face.

Furious, she stopped dancing and pried herself loose. She retreated, leaving the dance floor without looking back.

He grabbed her elbow from behind, halting her. Reflexively, she yanked her arm from his grasp and gave him the scariest don't-fuck-with-me look she could muster.

The shithead didn't get it.

She walked away, but he followed her, off the patio and back into the bar. She found herself pressed between a booth and the wall from the crush of people trying to get in and out of the bar. Justin was at her elbow again.

"They warned us about girls like you." Justin said in her ear.

"Like what?" Olivia's hackles were raised at being cornered and by his aggressive pursuit.

"Revolving doors," Justin said, barely concealing his disgust.

Olivia was beyond pissed now.

"A door you were just trying to step through, but it got slammed in your face. Didn't like that did you?" Olivia snapped at him. "If it isn't clear yet, let me make it crystal. Don't touch me. I'm not interested. Now leave me alone"

"Hey, buddy. I think she wants to be left alone."

Joel had snuck up on them; the crowd had parted to let him through. Olivia was surprised to see him out from behind the bar.

"But out," Justin said.

That was the wrong thing to say to Joel.

Olivia had seen Joel bounce guys before. Usually, he would escort them out, without any trouble. The more belligerent ones, he would twist and arm behind their back and haul them out. Most were too drunk and powerless to resist. She had never seen Joel get in a fight before.

Joel's arm moved faster than Olivia had thought those sono tubes could possibly go. His fist smashed Justin's face, sending a spurt of blood flying at Olivia. She squealed as droplets spattered her. She wasn't squeamish—she worked around plenty of blood—but it wasn't normally flying at her.

Justin did the worst of all possible things—he tried to fight back.

Joel swatted Justin's feeble punches away and slugged Justin twice more. And by golly did he connect—Justin looked like he had been swatted with a telephone pole. He collapsed to the floor. His nose and cheekbone were smashed and both lips were split. Olivia's gut did a flip when Justin spit out what looked like, a tooth.

The music stopped and lights came to full brightness. The patrons groaned and were generally confused; it was way too early for last call.

"Jesus Christ, Joel," Olivia said. "Did you have to be so rough?"

"Sorry, O. He looked like he was giving you trouble," Joel said.

"I was handling it," she said, peeved. "Get me ice and towels, before he bleeds out everywhere. And call an ambulance."

Joel looked irritated. "You're not with this loser are you?"

"No. But I am a nurse. I can't just let him die on your floor."

Joel got the ice and rags, and Olivia set to work staunching the flow of blood and icing down Justin's injuries. He was a bit out of it, making her wonder whether he also had a concussion.

The other bouncers moved in, cordoning off a circle around Olivia and Justin, giving them some breathing room. Justin looked up at her, confused. She found his tooth stuck to his pants. She wrapped it in a tissue and stuck it in his pocket.

"Your tooth is in your pocket," she said to him. "If you want it back in your head, remember to tell the doctor when you get to the hospital."

Justin nodded at her, but she wasn't sure if he would remember. Why did she even care? But she supposed she couldn't *not* care, she didn't like seeing people sick and injured. Being a nurse was about helping people heal—even if the patient was an asshole.

"What the hell!" Lauren yelled at her.

Olivia shrugged. Lieutenant. Beef was with Lauren, holding her hand. Upon recognizing his buddy, Lieutenant. Beef let out a whoop.

"Ha! Wish I could've seen that. He got leveled," Beef said.

Sometimes Olivia didn't understand these Navy guys at all.

The red lights of the ambulance, splashed in patterns on the walls. The paramedics made their way in through the patio with a gurney. Olivia gave them a run down of Justin's injuries and the suspected concussion, and they loaded him onto the gurney.

"We're bringing him over to NH, you want to come?" a paramedic asked her.

"God, no. I'm off duty," Olivia said with a shudder.

"Does he have any friends here that could go with him? It would make the admission easier," the paramedic asked.

"He came with a group," Olivia said, looking over to where Lauren and Beef had been, but they had disappeared back into the ground. *Shit.*

She really wanted the paramedics to just take him and be done with it, but she felt bad leaving the schmuck alone. She noticed that the police had arrived, but Joel had intercepted them and was chatting them up by the main entrance. Looking around, the rest of the Navy patrons seemed to have completely pulled out. She didn't spot a uniform anywhere.

So much for leaving no man behind, or was that the Army?

She didn't know. The only thing she was certain of was that right now she was the only person here that had any connection to Justin, however tenuous and acrimonious, which left her no choice.

"Alright. I'll go," Olivia said.

Chapter 6

Dr. Pretzel was on the mid-shift in the emergency room. 'Pretzel' wasn't Amelie Preizal's real name, just what they called her because it was too delightfully close to resist. And although she complained about its corniness, it didn't help her case that she was also wicked into Yoga.

Justin whimpered as Pretzel slid the needle through his lip, sewing the split back together. Justin's nose was broken, but it turned out Olivia had been wrong about his cheekbone being broken, though he did have a vicious cut, likely caused by one of Joel's rings. Pretzel had already patched that together. Justin's eyes were already developing dark circles under them; he was going to be raccooned for sure by morning. Tests for a concussion had turned out negative.

"You'll probably have some light scarring, but it should heal up fine, Champ," Pretzel said.

Justin grunted.

"You sure know how to pick 'em, O," Pretzel said.

"I did not pick him." Olivia protested. "We're not together."

"Whatever. Not any of my biz," Pretzel said. She took another stitch through Justin's lip. "Where's the other wonder twin?"

Olivia would have smacked Pretzel if she weren't stitching up a patient. She hated Pretzel's nickname for them, but Olivia guessed it beat being called a baked snack food all day.

To certain extent, Lauren and she did have superpowers—to attract the opposite sex, that is.

"At Black Orchid as far as I know, partying it up," Olivia said, sulkily.

Pretzel finished stitching Justin and tied off the suture. She clipped it and disposed of her gloves and waste in one of the biohazard bins.

"Back together again, Humpty," Pretzel said to Justin. "Use the ice." Pretzel pointed at the instant cold pack Justin had in his hand. He hastily raised it to his face. "I'm done here, you're free to go."

As Pretzel gathered her things and prepared to leave the room, she said to Olivia, "Good luck with that one, Red."

Olivia would've growled at her if she didn't feel so tired. She turned back to Justin.

"Alright, babysitting detail is over. You can get back to base on your own, right?" Olivia asked.

Justin nodded.

"Good," Olivia said.

"For what it's worth, I'm sorry," Justin said.

"Already forgotten," Olivia said. All had been forgotten, except for the teensy-weensy part where he had not-so-subtly insinuated she was a whore earlier. *That* she had mentally filed away. She felt a bit sorry for Justin. Joel really had overreacted. But he didn't fool around once he decided to bounce a guy, and Justin had misjudged that, just like he had misjudged her. She hoped Justin smartened up.

She made sure she had her clutch and keys still . . . damn . . . her car was still downtown. She was going to need a cab, too. She opened her clutch, but there was only $5 wrapped around her license; that wouldn't get her anywhere. Fat chance Lauren was going to come and pick her up. She could hoof it back to the apartment, but it was late, dark and her shoes sucked. But there was another alternative, even if she was loath to take it.

"See you around," Olivia said and gave a little wave to Justin. Hopefully that would be the last time she saw him, but she had a sneaking suspicion that they would be seeing more of each other if Lauren had shacked up with Beef. Olivia hoped not, but it was looking likely, which was problematical. Lauren's initial taste tended to be imprudent. Olivia could usually head such problems off at the pass by giving Lauren a wake-up call. It wasn't to say Olivia was any better at choosing for herself, because, god knows, Lauren had saved her a couple times as well. Tonight's screwy-ness had mangled the usual routine.

She went to the desk; Seth Little was on shift, one of the few male nurses at the hospital. He was typing furiously on the computer, pausing only to brush his shaggy brown hair out of his eyes, to look at the folders and papers spread on the desk in front of him. He was processing claims paperwork the hospital would submit the insurance companies and Medicare to get paid.

"Hey," Olivia said.

"Hey back," Seth responded, eyes still focused on his work. He looked up from his paperwork, and did a double take. "Whoa. You just come from a strip club?"

"Very funny. No," Olivia said. "It's been a strange night."

"I take it not, 'Ha, ha' funny?" Seth said, teasing.

Olivia just grinned her *I'm-going-to-bite-your-face-off-if-you-keep-it-up* grin at him, which made Seth grin even bigger, gut he didn't provoke her further. "My car is still downtown and I'm broke. Are there any free beds?"

"Or course," Seth said and turned to look at the occupancy chart. "Examination rooms eight through twelve are free. Want some spare blankets and pillows?"

"Awesome," Olivia said.

* * *

Olivia walked down the hall, her arms laden with extra blankets and pillows. She hated the mattresses on the exam room beds, but would make do tonight. Her feet hurt and all she wanted to do was crash. The quicker she could put the crazy night behind her, the better. Tomorrow, she would walk back to the apartment and scold Lauren first for not waiting for her to go the Rhino and then for leaving her with Justin. Not that it would do much good, but at least it would feel good to vent on her

"Fancy meeting you here," Andrew said.

He was standing in his doorway, fully dressed, and looking just as delicious as he had been in his johnnie. Olivia's arms were full, making wiping drool from her mouth an impossible task. She had been so caught up in her thoughts she had nearly walked past him, oblivious.

Recovering from her stupor, she said, "And you. Small world."

She found she was blinking rapidly at him, and had to look away. But then she was looking all around like an idiot. Finally, she looked back at him, her cheeks felt flushed.

"Looking for a place to crash?" Andrew said, pointing at her armful of bedding.

"I don't think that would be a good idea," she said, but her clit, twitching, voted for the sleepover.

"Funny, I thought it sounded like an excellent idea."

Andrew smiled at her and she wanted to melt. If she stood here much longer, she was going to cave.

"I work here. It's inappropriate," she stalled.

"That didn't stop you earlier."

"Earlier I was a bit too persuadable."

"You know what I think," Andrew said, stepping closer to her.

She felt herself growing weak in his shadow, like he was her kryptonite.

"What?" she said, swallowing the spit that had accumulated in her mouth.

He leaned in and kissed her full on the lips, destroying her defenses. She kissed him back, hungrily pulling at his lips. Their tongues darted in out of each other's mouths.

"Not in the hall," she said between breaths.

He stepped backwards, drawing her into his room. She kicked the door closed, behind her. Their kissing grew more vigorous, her lips already bruising from his forceful kisses. He swept the bedding out of her arms and into a heap on the floor. Their hands scoured each other, trying to touch every inch of their bodies, without breaking the frenetic rhythm of their kissing.

His rough fingers found the ties of her shirt. Pulling them, he stripped the garment from her, exposing her breasts. Her nipples were hard and erect. She was eager for him to suck on them, but he continued to kiss her, instead stroking her breasts and cupping them gently with his warm hands. The sensation sent a chill up her spine and she cooed in delight.

She worked the buttons on his shirt and pushed it down, off of his shoulders, exposing his strong arms and chest. She ran her fingers down his chest, gently dragging her nails across his tanned skin. He moaned at her touch.

He scooped her up in his arms and carried her to the bed. He gently set her down, kissing her again. He gripped the waistband and pulled her pants down, over her hips, down her thighs and calves. She pulled her feet free of the cuffs and he discarded them, then kicked off her shoes and sent them over the side of the mattress.

Andrew leaned over her and resumed kissing her again, leaving her a bit frustrated—she needed him in her now. But Andrew still had his pants on and didn't seem in any hurry to jump her. He kissed her repeatedly, working his way slowly down her neck. Cupping her breasts, he brought the left nipple into his mouth and sucked it gently. Olivia gasped at the sensation. He switched from the left to sucking on the right nipple, sending more ripples of pleasure through her. He laid a series of kisses down her stomach and around her belly button. She was wet with anticipation as he alternated kisses on her pelvis. His fingers played with her bush, making her even wetter. She was sure there must be a wet spot on the bed already, she was so amped up.

She spread herself open, eagerly anticipating his touch, but he pulled away. She almost cried out in frustration at his teasing. He pushed her legs together and kissed the tops of her knees. He watched her as his lips touched her. She wanted to scream at him to get to work, but she stifled the thought; he was in control of her pleasure again.

"Please," she begged, shifting seductively. It was all the coaxing Andrew needed.

Separating her legs, he kissed the inside of her thighs, alternating sides while slowly working his way to her pussy, even kissing the crease where her leg joined her body. Her clit was engorged and ached for him. As if sensing her need, he finally descended on her, taking her plump button into his mouth. He sucked on her slowly, working the little knob, round and round with his tongue. Olivia gasped, writhing as zingers of pleasure danced through her body.

The pressure built and built, as Andrew kept working her clit in his mouth. It was agony and ecstasy rolled together again. One moment she couldn't take it any longer, the next she couldn't get enough. Unable to contain herself any longer, her body spasmed as the orgasm pulsed through her core and radiated out to her extremities. She moaned uncontrollably, as each wave of pleasure coursed through her quivering body.

Andrew stood up and shucked the rest of his clothes. His cock was erect; the tip glistened. Straddling her, he guided himself into her. She was so slick, he slid right in, filing her up. She had a moment of worry that he might think she was too loose. Looking at him dispelled the thought. His eyes were riveted on her face. The expression on his face had one message—he hungered for her.

His thrusts started slow, but quickly sped up. His strokes never shortened, as he seemingly endeavored for her to feel every inch of him sliding in and out of her. She brought her knees up, angling herself to take as much of him in her as she could. He lengthened his stroke even more, the ridge of his penis popping her opening with each thrust, stimulating her in ways she didn't think possible.

His body shuddered and he skipped a stroke, climaxing in her.

"Don't stop," Olivia begged as she could feel herself rising again.

With renewed vigor, Andrew resumed his relentless pace.

"Almost there," she said encouragingly, between panted breaths.

And amazingly she was. Her body was cresting again. She was mewling; her second orgasm was so frustratingly close, but just out of reach. She looked up at Andrew and found he was studying her intently, his deep brown eyes seemingly searching for a way to look inside her head. She held his gaze as it sent her over the edge. As the pleasure ebbed away, her body fell flaccid underneath him. She was completely and thoroughly spent.

* * *

Andrew rolled off of Olivia. She was limp as a rag doll. Her body was hot and slick with sweat, mixed with their juices. The scent cloyed at his nostrils, intoxicating in the current context, a slap in the face under any other. He stroked her, gently, letting her catch her breath and cool down from their passion. The woman was unlike any he had ever had.

Olivia turned on her side and nuzzled against him, resting her head in the crook of his neck and curling a leg over him—and the most otherworldly feeling of content swamped his roller coaster emotions of the last twenty-four hours. He squeezed her to his side and she responded in kind.

She kissed his jaw, a tender, short peck.

A tear trickled down his cheek. He brushed it away quickly with a free hand. The thought he might have died earlier unnerved him. Tia had saved him. She had led him away from certain death for a reason. Could that reason be this woman? Amanda would have a problem with that. He snorted at the thought.

"What's so funny?" Olivia asked.

"Just this whole situation," he said, "of how we met."

"I have to go," Olivia said, tersely.

She jumped out the bed and started searching for her hastily-discarded clothes.

"Stay." He tried to persuade her. "No one will be the wiser," he said, sensing her fear.

He propped himself up on an elbow and admired her silhouetted nude form, scrounging around the darkened room.

"No, I'm supposed to be a professional. This is completely out of bounds," she said, panic, fear, and anger tainting her words.

She had found her pants and was doing a one-legged dance trying to pull them on. Her breasts jounced, almost distracting him from the realization that she was intent on leaving until she angrily tied her shirt back on. Finding her shoes, finally, she slipped into them.

"Don't be angry with yourself," he said, trying to shift the blame.

"I am angry," She snapped back at him, "don't tell me how to feel."

She stormed out of the room, but returned moments later—but not she realized her mistake in leaving him. She picked up the spare blankets and pillows she had been carrying earlier and stormed back out. He thought to chase after her, but restrained himself. She was afraid of them getting caught together. He would wait, and seek her out tomorrow.

He pulled the blankets snug around him and felt himself drift off. For the first time in longer than he could remember, his head was clear, anxiety didn't permeate him.

Chapter 7

Andrew woke the next morning completely refreshed. In fact, he felt better than he'd felt in a year. The change was so radical for him; he had trouble believing he had lived like a recluse for so long. Then again, he hadn't come out of unscathed had he? The turmoil his life had been in had nearly cost him everything. He'd tried to submerge himself in work, only to find himself drowning in grief, day after day. For the first time, he felt like he could go on. Not that the pain of losing Tia was any less; it just somehow seemed manageable now.

Reluctantly, he had to give the doctor some credit. He was loath to do it, but he wasn't one to ignore facts that were plainly in his face. Heriberto had influenced him where none previously could. And the nurse, Olivia. Just thinking about her got his blood pumping.

There was a light rap at the door and someone entered, pushing a cart. His hopes that it was Olivia were dashed—it was the attendant, with the breakfast trays

"Good morning," the woman said. "How are we doing today? Hungry, I hope."

He was hungry, but not for food. Hungry to get out of here. Hungry to find Olivia. Hungry to peel off whatever she was wearing and work her over until she begged him to stop. He tried to clear his mind before he built a pup tent in the sheets with an erection.

"Thanks. Leave it there. I'm not quite ready for it yet," he said.

She did as he asked and excused herself from the room.

Andrew threw the covers off and got in the shower. He rinsed quickly and dried off, then got dressed and hit the nurse's call button. One way or another, he was getting out of here today.

He checked his phone for the first time since Olivia had retrieved it. Eight bajillion missed calls from Amanda and work. He deleted Amanda's voicemail without even listening to it; it would be more of the same and he had had it with her. Plus listening would be downright painful, as they likely got progressively shriller.

He was about to delete the text messages in one fell swoop, when the ridiculousness of what she was saying caught his eye. Now he wished he had listened to a couple of those voicemails before wiping them out. She had definitely gone off the deep end, swearing that they were meant to be together till the end of time, she would shave the redheaded cunt's head, and invoking Tia. The first made him laugh, the second confused him that she would even know about Olivia—he had only just met her himself—and the third made him angry. She had no right to use Tia to manipulate him anymore.

He wiped Amanda's messages and turned to the business messages he had missed. He was in the middle of returning a call when Dr. Heriberto let himself into the room. Andrew finished up the call and put the phone away.

"It's good to see you scheduling jobs," Heriberto said. "Sorry, I didn't mean to pry."

"Things need to get done," Andrew replied with a shrug. He put his phone away and focused his attention on Heriberto.

"Does it make you feel good?" Heriberto asked.

"Huh?" Andrew replied intelligently, confused as to what he was even talking about.

"Working." Heriberto clarified.

Andrew thought about it for a moment, but it was true. He didn't work just to forget; it also provided focus and accomplishment. "Yes, actually. It does."

"You sound a bit surprised," Heriberto said.

"I hadn't really thought about it before. I've used work to *avoid* thinking about things for so long that I forgot I actually do like it," Andrew said.

"We all do," Heriberto said, then adding, "avoid things, that is. But sooner or later it catches up to us all. How we deal with them when they do is important. It's good to have relationships you can turn to then, regardless of whether they are formal. Family, close friends—American men are terrible at them. Find yourself some friends that you can talk with about important things—more than just football and beer. Use the Samaritans until you can build your own network. It'll make you happier. It'll help you through hard times."

"Thank you," Andrew said.

And, surprisingly, he genuinely meant it.

"I'm not seeing any signs you are a danger to yourself or anyone. If anything, you look reinvigorated," Heriberto said, seeming mildly confused at Andrew's seemingly overnight transformation.

Andrew wondered briefly whether Heriberto might think he was bipolar.

Of course, Olivia had provided him some uniquely intense therapy last night—a remedy he wanted to avail himself of again.

"I do. I am," Andrew said. "I've done a lot of thinking since our talk, yesterday."

"Good. I don't feel like we need to keep you under observation anymore, so I'm discharging you. If you are having feelings of hopelessness again, please remember there are people who care. Give the hotline a call before you make any rash decisions."

Andrew nodded.

"The nurse, Olivia, how might I find her?" Andrew asked. "I need to thank her for getting my stuff."

"I don't think she's in today. Of course, if you send anything to the hospital addressed to her or me, we'll make sure she gets it," Heriberto explained.

Andrew was disappointed, because aside from the hospital, he didn't have any way to contact Olivia. Maybe that would be enough, but she had been fairly upset; and Andrew knew that if word of their multiple trysts got out, it might have severe consequences for her. He would have to be discrete.

The thought flashed briefly through his head that she might not even want to see him anymore; that the line that they had crossed was such a violation of her conscience that she couldn't see him without getting sick to her stomach or something. He pushed the thought out of his head; there would be no negativity to the extent he could control it from here on out. A resolution of sorts he had decided just now to follow.

The thought that Olivia might be sick with worry about their one-night stand, he did find amusing; if only for the contrast with Amanda. Was there anything that would have ever made Amanda anxious, ethically? It wasn't very charitable, he knew, but their history together was so complicated. More complicated than any relationship had a right to be and survive.

But that was in the past now.

He gathered his things and checked himself out.

Life started again today.

* * *

"What the fuck, Andy," Kristin said, pissing and moaning at him. "Where the hell have you been?"

Andrew hadn't seen his sister this mad since their father died and left the controlling stake of the business with him.

He couldn't explain what had happened over the last couple of days, though. If she found out, she would have been to the courthouse faster than, well, anything he could think of, to place his share of the company in some sort of conservatorship, effectively giving her control of the company.

He didn't know why they couldn't get along in running the company together. He was more than willing to let her wield a substantial amount of authority. She practically ran the back office, while he managed the crews, equipment, and scheduling. She even had significant input on contracts, operations, and general business strategy. The one thing he didn't let her do, which really stuck in her craw, was meet with customers.

She had a lot of Dad in her—she worked hard and believed in the company—but she also had a temper and a bad habit of pissing the wrong people off. The main difference was that Dad recognized his shortcomings and had trusted people to make a sanity check against before he let that famous temper loose. Kristen skipped that step and managed to step the temper out far too frequently. Andrew was convinced it was that combination of temperament combined with Dad's old-fashioned, misogynistic upbringing that led him to leave Andrew in control of the company.

He probably should have given Kristen enough shares to make her an equal partner, something he told himself he would have done at the time given the chance, but when she contested the will before their father had been buried for even a month had left a sour taste in his mouth.

Sometimes he wished she were just greedy. It would be easier to handle. He could pay her off and be done with it. But Kristen wanted to control the company, and whether she knew it or not—and he doubted she did—she was a bad fit for it.

Maybe someday he would get sick of the drama and ask her to buy him out. But he also worried about his Dad's legacy. He didn't want the company to go into the toilet. It wouldn't happen immediately. Kristen was too good for that; but over time, she would lose contracts and Medina Tree Service would get hollowed out like a rotten log until it collapsed on itself, something he couldn't bear to witness.

"Quit fucking smiling at me, before I come over there and wipe it from your face." She literally huffed at him.

It was hard to not smile, and her anger made it even harder. As much as she could grate against him, she was still his sister.

"And you've got to do something about Amanda. I'm not managing that bitch for you any more. It's not our job to make excuses for you and run interference. Be a fucking man and handle her," Kristen said, slamming the files she had been waving at him on the desk for added emphasis.

"I'll take care of her," Andrew said. "She won't bother anyone here any more."

Kristen was about to let off another round at him, but his answer had caught her off-guard. He knew she had been expecting him to defend Amanda; that's what he did. At least that's what he had always done in the past.

But that was the past now, and it was time to move on.

"Thanks," Kristen said, lamely. "So," she continued circling back to her first topic more calmly, "what was all the incommunicado about?"

"I took an unexpected trip," he said, reflecting on the last couple of days and trying to figure out the best way to explain his absence vaguely, without alarming her. He wanted to share how he was feeling with Kristen, but wasn't quite sure how to go about it. "I just needed a couple of days to myself, to clear my head. I'm back now."

"Oh god, I'm so shitty for getting on your case," Kristen said, covering her mouth with a hand. "It's been a year hasn't it?"

Andrew nodded. His chest and throat tightened at the oblique reference to Tia. The pain felt fresh and hot.

Did the pain ever get better? he had asked Heriberto.

No, we just get better at managing it, Heriberto had said.

He choked out a laugh that Kristen mistook for crying.

"I'm so sorry, Andy," she said. "Take time off. Take the whole fucking month off. We can handle things here."

Andrew took a couple of deep breaths and pulled his shit together before answering her.

"I appreciate it. I do," he said, meeting her gaze. "But work gives me something to keep my mind occupied."

She nodded acceptance, but said the opposite. "You can deal with things however you want, hon; but work isn't useful for healing."

"So I'm realizing," he said, then quickly changing topics before she probed for more detail, "Tell me about the new solicitation. Should we bid on it?"

The distraction worked perfectly. Kristen picked up the folder she had been waving around and broke into her spiel on the merits and pitfalls of the solicitation, the gist of which was a three-year contract to maintain the Northeast's main trunk lines, which, last time he had seen them, were long overdue for trimming. During the last hurricane, customers had been stranded without power for weeks as line crews repaired the tree-felled lines, the damage caused primarily by years of neglect or maintenance. The ensuing outrage, stirred up by news outlets and local pols, had apparently gotten someone's attention, which meant quite an opportunity for the company. Northeast was looking for one tree service company to award the contract to, and few could match Medina's capability.

That is, if they could make the numbers work.

Number-crunching was Kristen's specialty. The more she laid out the costs versus the commitment, the more skeptical he became that Northeast would be willing to pay their fee.

There had to be some angle he was missing. *Why now? Why this proposal?*

He peppered Kristen with questions and scenarios, which she deftly answered or deflected with evidence to the contrary of his concern, and he actually found he was enjoying the strategy discussion with her; the first in a long time. How he had lived so hollow for so long, he didn't know. Only on the precipice of death did he realize what he actually had.

"What," Kristen said, "have I got something on my face?"

She reached up to her cheek.

"No," he said, laughing. "I'm just glad to be back, that's all."

"Are you on drugs or something, you fucking weirdo?" she said.

He laughed even harder.

They wrapped up the session and Kristen left to draft up a formal bid. In the meantime, Andrew agreed to dig into the scuttlebutt on the solicitation and, if he could, reconnect with Olivia. Only half a day had passed and the thought of spending the night without her tonight made him frustrated. Just thinking about her now got his mouth watering and blood pumping. But short of going back to the hospital, he didn't have any idea how he would get in touch with her.

Maybe it didn't have to be complicated, though? He could do as Heriberto had suggested, send a message to the hospital, and let her decide to contact him. If she didn't, he would have his answer, as disappointing as it may be to him.

If she did respond to his message though . . . , well, the thought of it had his mouth watering all over again. He tried to not get too excited in case she rebuffed him.

How to send the message was another matter. If it were too discreet, it might get lost or she might not think he wanted to see her again. Too attention-getting or blunt, and it could embarrass her—or revive that angry streak she had displayed for him if she thought their liaison could be discovered. He pulled a sheet of paper from his notepad and set to work crafting a note. Spontaneous words weren't his strong suit, but with some time and effort, he thought he could craft something subtle and persuasive enough to entice her to contact him.

Chapter 8

Olivia reluctantly decided it was time to get up despite the very compelling fact that the covers were snugged around her perfectly. She was loath to disrupt the coziness, but she had slept in far too late; it was almost eleven in the morning. It was her day off, so she could spend it anyway she chose, but she would regret spending the entire day in bed.

She threw the covers off her body and sat up, giving herself a good cat-stretch. She was revitalized. She barely remembered the last time she had a night's sleep that was as perfect—and on a hospital examination bed at that. She was sure it would have scored a ten out-of-ten if judging sleep were a contest. At least she scored it that way.

God, she felt good.

The night had been pure insanity—psycho ex-girlfriends, bar fight, trip to the emergency room and amazing sex, not once but twice—the amazing sex that is. It definitely took the prize for craziest night she had ever had. And to a certain extent it wasn't over—she was still in the hospital, and now had to surreptitiously leave in her clubbing outfit to do the walk of shame back to her apartment; except this time she would definitely have a spring in her step.

She checked her phone, nothing from Lauren. Some wingman she was. Hopefully Lauren had had as delightfully stimulating night as she had, but somehow she doubted anything could have compared to Andrew's tenderizing of her body. The memory of their encounters awakened the desire in her again; something she wasn't quite used to feeling.

Weren't only guys supposed to feel horny like this?

She hoped in the shower and rinsed off, in part, to clean the club scum and sex off of her and, in part, to distract herself from thinking about Andrew. Toweling off dry, she stuffed herself back into her club outfit and thought about how best to sneak out of the hospital without bumping into anyone she knew. A task that was further complicated by the fact that a shift change was underway.

She poked her head out the door and looked down the hall. Someone, probably Seth, had hung a "do not disturb" sign on her door, which she would be eternally grateful for. Heriberto was walking down the hall. She tried to shrink back out of sight, but he spotted her and gave her a wave.

Damn.

She couldn't very well avoid him now. She stepped out of the room and promptly saw his expression sour before quickly recovering.

"I thought you had the day off?" he asked, checking her out with a perplexed expression on his face.

"I am. I got trapped here after an emergency last night," Olivia said.

"Lauren?" Heriberto asked, concerned.

"No, she's fine as far as I know," Olivia said. "Bar fight. I ended up with babysitting duty, and then it got to be too late to walk home."

Heriberto nodded and turned to go.

Olivia sighed in relief; she just wanted to make her escape now.

"Oh, before I forget," Heriberto said, turning back to her.

What now?

"Someone asked for you," Heriberto said, clearly holding the suspense by not telling her who.

Olivia shrugged her shoulders and put on a questioning look.

"Andrew Medina, the patient that came in yesterday that you were kind enough to run that errand for." Heriberto smiled approvingly at her.

Olivia stiffened, bracing herself for the dressing-down that was about to begin before he fired her and threatened to report her to the board. To think she had been so weak and stupid to throw everything away? And for what? An exceptional roll in the hay with a stranger with mental problems? She should have been the one involuntarily held, because clearly she was insane, too.

"Andrew was very grateful for your help last night and he wanted to thank you," Heriberto said.

Olivia was taken aback. They hadn't been found out. She wasn't being fired.

"That's great," she said nervously.

"I'm grateful, too," Heriberto said. "It was at the end of your shift and you didn't need to. I appreciate your going the extra mile."

If only he knew how far exactly she'd gone.

"Is he still here?" Olivia asked before she could stifle the question. She wanted to slap herself for asking. Andrew was off-limits. Although her lapse in judgment had been possibly the best sex she had ever experienced in her life—and quite possibly the afterlife—she couldn't let it happen again.

"No, I released him this morning."

Olivia felt a pang of sadness at having missed Andrew leaving, which she tried to push out of her mind.

"Anyway, I'll let you be on your way," Heriberto said.

He turned a moment later. "By the way, does your mother know you dress like this?"

"It's none of her business. Or yours," Olivia growled

Heriberto held up his hands in surrender and continued on his way.

* * *

Olivia let herself into the apartment. Lauren and Lieutenant. Beef were sitting at the kitchen table, looking as if they had just gotten up from bed not too long ago themselves. Lauren was dressed in sweats and a t-shirt, her hair pulled hastily through a scrunchy. Beef was in his disheveled dress whites. Obviously they had spent the night here, which Olivia was glad she'd missed. Lauren tended to overdue the orgasmic screaming, in Olivia's opinion, which even the old plaster walls couldn't seem to muffle. In reality, it was only annoying if Olivia was alone.

Beef was more attractive than she had given credit for last night. Although everything about him seemed overly burly, he was very rugged-looking with dark brown hair and genial eyes, which reminded her of Andrew. She pushed the thought of Andrew out of her mind, to focus on the task at hand: the morning-after assessment. A stark reality-check to ensure they hadn't made a terrible, drunken choice the night before. If she had to place Beef from anywhere in the country, he seemed a Midwesterner.

Olivia really wished she had managed to get Beef's name earlier. Now she was going to have to stumble through embarrassing gyrations of nicknames and other tricks to avoid admitting she couldn't remember his name.

"Hey, hon," Lauren said. "What happened to you last night?"

Olivia wanted to take Lauren's head off, but decided against it in light of the company. Lauren continued on without even bothering to let Olivia answer, adding further to her annoyance.

"You remember Chris?" Lauren said lazily waving a hand at him.

Off the hook.

"Of course," Olivia said. "Sorry we didn't get much of a chance to chat."

Olivia extended a hand. Chris took it gently and gave it a chaste shake. His hands were rough with calluses, just like Andrew's. Again she forced Andrew from her mind. The calluses were surprising on an lieutenant. By this time, their hands had usually gone soft from too much deskwork. Her surprise at his grip must have shown.

"Weight lifting," Chris said, explaining.

Lauren looked a little put-out, like Olivia had stolen her surprise.

"I compete," Chris added.

"He's being bashful. You're competing for the Olympic Team," Lauren said, smiling approvingly. Chris beamed at her.

"That's ambitious. But how?" Olivia said.

"The Navy will grant me leave to join the team if I qualify. It's great publicity for them," Chris said. "But first I need to qualify. In the meantime, I still have a Navy job to do."

"So where'd you and Justin disappear off to?" Lauren said.

Olivia gave her a *you've-got-to-be-kidding-me* look. "Let's not even go there."

Lauren looked confused and gave her a snot-look back. Obviously, she had been so drunk last night and enamored with Chris that she couldn't even remember where Olivia had disappeared to. It was aggravating and upsetting. Not that anything bad had happened to Olivia, but it was rude that she got left without even a call or text from Lauren about where she was or if Olivia was okay.

"I've gotta get out of this outfit," Olivia said excusing herself. "Nice to see you again, Chris."

Olivia scurried out of the kitchen and into her room. She didn't intend to slam her bedroom door, but it banged loudly as it got away from her. A surge of guilt and shame passed through her.

Why'd she feel like a spoiled teenager?

It wasn't until Olivia was alone that she realized that she wasn't really angry with Lauren, but with herself for weakly succumbing to Andrew. If Lauren hadn't enticed her into going out last night or had gotten one of Justin's so-called buddies to travel with him to the hospital instead of her, she would have avoided seeing Andrew again.

Of course, it wasn't lost on Olivia that the first go-round with Andrew was entirely her fault. Even now, the thought of him running his hands over her body got her temperature up. She threw her dirty clothes into the hamper with more force than necessary, trying to distract herself from these unwanted feelings that kept washing over her.

If only she could stop thinking about Andrew.

As Olivia pulled on some clothes, she caught the sight of her angry face on her closet mirror, which caused her pause. She needed to calm and collect herself. What was done was done, and there was no sense regretting anything. The whole thing could blow away without anyone the wiser.

A soft knock emanated from her door.

"Yep," Olivia said.

The door creaked open, revealing Lauren.

"Chris is gone," Lauren said. She stood in the doorway, a concerned expression on her face. "Wanna talk?"

Olivia clasped her hands to her face as if she could wipe away the events from her head. She could settle for the memory. She dropped her hands and looked at Lauren.

"I'm sorry," Olivia said. "I was rude out there."

Lauren nodded.

"What happened last night?" Lauren asked. "We turned around a moment to get Chris's crew, and you guys disappeared into the ambulance. One of the guys got a message from Justin and picked him up from the hospital. I thought you guys were together this whole time."

Now Olivia felt even more stupid. If she hadn't felt pressured by the paramedic, she could have avoided the trip last night. Worse, she could have gotten a ride back home.

"Justin was a jerk. I left him at the hospital," Olivia said.

"Where'd you go?" Lauren said. A confused expression was plastered on her face. Obviously, Olivia hadn't come home last night.

"I slept at the hospital. Seth was on duty and gave me my pick of the open rooms," Olivia explained.

"You nitwit, you should've called me," Lauren said. "I'd have come get you."

Olivia gave her a skeptical look.

"Shut up!" Lauren protested. "No way would I have left you there for Chris. Come on? Give me more credit than that. I just met the guy. Sure, I wouldn't have let you hear the end of it for screwing up my groove, but ho's before bro's any day."

Olivia smiled.

Before she could resist, Lauren gave her a hug.

"Okay, stop it," Olivia said.

Lauren let her go, laughing.

"So, tell me about Chris," Olivia said inviting the distraction she desperately needed to keep her thoughts from wandering back to Andrew.

Lauren didn't let her down.

* * *

The next day, Olivia was making her rounds at the hospital when she was paged.

"Nurse Bennett, Nurse Bennett. Please report to the admissions desk for an important delivery." Lauren's voice was distinctive over the intercom and did she detect a bit of mirth in it? Her phrasing was definitely unusual and what kind of 'delivery' would she be receiving at the hospital anyway?

She turned her cart around and proceeded back to the nurse's station to drop it off before heading down to the admissions desk.

"Nurse Bennett, Nurse Bennett. Please report to the admissions desk for an important delivery," Lauren said in a soothing monotone again.

Hold on, already!

This time she definitely heard laughter in the background. Something was definitely up. She dropped off the cart and marked the chart where she had left off. Although they had the latest computer-fandangled system, old habits died hard, and she still preferred having a hard copy list with her. She left the nurses station and took the stairs down to the lobby and admissions desk.

Gathered around the desk were Lauren and the other crew of nurses working her shift. Pretzel was there as well. All of the them sporting shit-eating grins. She couldn't help but hide the perplexed look on her face, which made the group of grinning baboons in front of her almost lose it. Strike that, Pretzel already had, practically doubling over with laughter.

Then she saw why. Three vases of flowers were arranged on the admissions desk. She hadn't seen them earlier because Patrick Sullivan's girth was hiding them. Even Patrick, the security guard, looked like he was in on the joke, whatever it was.

"What's going on?" Olivia said once she was within earshot of the group.

Lauren keyed the mic again. "Delivery for Nurse Bennett."

"Cut that out," Olivia said. "You guys are causing a scene."

Olivia was suddenly aware of the patients and their families in the lobby glancing over at the spectacle.

"Here you go," Lauren said handing her one of the vases.

Olivia felt a little tingle in her belly. Regardless of the attempts of her coworkers to embarrass her, it still felt good to get flowers. The bouquet an explosion of pinks and purples, filled with lilacs, miniature and full-sized roses, and sweet peas, framed with baby's breath.

It was gorgeous.

She pulled the card from its holder and popped it open.

Thinking of you.

-Tyler

"Not that its any of your business, but since you're all on your tiptoes, it's from Tyler," Olivia said. Her cheeks grew warm at his gesture. At the same time, she really needed to end it, but this made it harder to do. She couldn't lead him on, though.

Olivia turned to go.

"Hold on there you vixen," Pretzel said.

Olivia turned back confused.

"You forgot this one," Lauren said, handing her the next vase.

The bouquet was filled with daisies, red dahlias, and purple snapdragons, with larkspurs lurking among the larger flowers. It was as gorgeous as the other bouquet. Olivia pulled the card from its holder and hastily opened it.

For what its worth, I'm sorry and thanks.

-Justin

Olivia's nose crinkled with disgust at seeing his name.

"Come on, we're dying to know," Lauren said.

"Justin," Olivia said with disapproval.

Olivia looked with dread and anticipation at the third bouquet sitting on the admissions desk—Red roses.

"I knew there was more between you two," Pretzel said, doing a fist pump.

"We're not together," Olivia protested, which just made Pretzel laugh more.

"And it looks like you've already guessed, this one is for you, too," Lauren said.

Lauren handed Olivia the last vase.

Chapter 9

Olivia plucked the card without taking any time to truly appreciate the last bouquet; the anticipation peaking in her until she could barely stand it. She ripped open the envelope, freeing the card.

Flipping it open, she read:

I'd like to see you again.

-Andrew

A phone number was scrawled beneath his name, she presumed was his.

Olivia's gut churned with a curious mix of pleasure and anxiety. If she had been a bit pink with embarrassment before, she was now full red.

"Ahem," Lauren said, grabbing Olivia's attention.

Looking up, Olivia noticed everyone was focused on her, waiting with bated breath for her to reveal the third admirer's name—something she had no intention of revealing to any of them. Both because she was beginning to not enjoy the "friendly" ribbing she was getting or the fact that if they, or at least if Pretzel, found out who the sender was, it might get her canned.

Instead, Olivia pocketed Andrew's card and smiled. She looked back down at Andrew's bouquet and admired it for the first time. It was filled with two-dozen red roses accented with baby's breath—nothing that guys hadn't sent girls before. The arrangement had an intoxicating effect on her. It was a bit overkill, but she had never received two-dozen roses from anyone before and found herself actually swooning. Maybe it was the combination of receiving all three bouquets back to back? She wasn't quite sure, but she sure as hell was enjoying the feeling of being wanted. She clutched the vase to her chest and started walking away.

"Hey!" the crowd catcalled her in unison, as if they'd been practicing, but she ignored them.

"Patrick, send the other two to the intensive care unit," Olivia called out behind her.

Let them chew on that!

Patrick *yes ma'am'd* her and added a small salute.

"You're killing us," Lauren called out after Olivia.

"Oh, a lady doesn't kiss and tell," Olivia said, casting her voice with a fake Victorian tone. Looking over her shoulder, she batted her eyes at her hecklers.

"You're no lady, Red," Pretzel said, jokingly. "More like a professional juggler."

Olivia ignored their taunts and escaped from the lobby with Andrew's roses. Her pulse was pounding as she took the stairs up to her assigned floor, but not from the exertion. She was thrilled to receive Andrew's gift and at having eluded everyone's scrutiny. Sure, Lauren would corner her later; but Lauren she could trust, although she felt like being very secretive now. Even if Lauren did corner her, she might just keep the knowledge of Andrew to herself.

She grabbed her cart and resumed her rounds where she had left off.

She couldn't help, but think of the strange situation while working, though, and her thoughts kept drifting back to her predicament. She would need to call Tyler and end it for good. She didn't want him thinking he still had a chance with her. He needed to have some closure and move on. It sucked, but she couldn't have him sending her gifts, and the last thing she need was him to fly out unannounced to visit her.

As for Justin, well, he could go fuck himself. He had been a drunken asshole that night, but first impressions were hard to get over. She had no interest in communicating with him. Maybe she could relay a message though Lauren and Chris that she wasn't interested. Under normal circumstance, not responding would be accepted as "not interested," but after the other night's problems she couldn't be sure he wasn't completely tone deaf.

Andrew's phone number burned at the back of her head and at the tips of her fingers. She found herself wanting to dig out her phone and call him or at least send a message. She couldn't do that, though. He was off-limits. Of course, just thinking that made her want him even more, which made her think about the sex they had together, which made her sweaty.

To be on the safe side, she pulled out her phone and powered it off, lest she was tempted to call him. She rethought that when she realized someone important might try to get in touch with her, forcing her to turn it back on.

Of course, her agitation only got worse once she had completed her rounds of the floor.

She pulled out Andrew's card, but couldn't get herself to destroy it. She put it back in her pocket . . . then took it out . . . then put it back in.

She felt like a kid with a nickel in penny candy store, unable to make a decision.

Instead she decided to call Tyler. That would be a sufficiently shitty exercise to cool her jets.

He picked up on the first ring.

"Hey!" Tyler said, with a cheerfulness that made Olivia feel even shittier.

"Hey back," Olivia said. "Thanks for the flowers."

* * *

Tyler had taken it much better than she'd feared, or at least controlled whatever emotions he was willing to reveal over the phone with remarkable self-restraint, but at least it was done now. Unfortunately, it didn't quite have the effect on her that she had intended. Instead of feeling like dogshit and wanting to crawl into a bucket of Häagen-Dazs, she felt freed; freed to call Andrew. She wanted to hurl her phone, but managed to stuff it back into a pocket where it set to smoldering a hole in her pants.

Why couldn't she control herself? Was she hell-bent on self-destructive behavior or did this man just bring it out in her?

She restocked the supply cabinets in the empty rooms. Then restocked all the occupied rooms.

Upon returning to the nurse's station, Lauren was waiting for her.

"Okay so who's the mystery man?" Lauren demanded.

Olivia stammered trying to think of someway to avoid the question.

"Come on, O," Lauren said. "It's me." Lauren pointed to herself, as if Olivia needed a visual cue to know who Lauren was referring to.

"Joel," Olivia blurted.

"Joel?" Lauren looked confused. "Joel, the bartender, sent you flowers?" Lauren looked incredulous.

"Yeah, Joel," Olivia said, trying to convince even herself. "Is there any other? He felt really bad about punching Justin's lights out and the flowers were his way of making it up to me and how I had to go to the hospital and everything." The lie tumbled out of Olivia easier than she thought it would.

"Joel," Lauren said, looking as if the concept that he might have sent Olivia flowers violated the laws of nature or physics. "Roses, though?"

"It was a little over the top, wasn't it?" Olivia said.

"He's not going to hear the end of this from me," Lauren said, smiling.

Olivia's face fell; this wasn't how it was supposed to go.

"Don't do that. He's really embarrassed about it," Olivia said.

"Joel?" Lauren said, disbelievingly.

"Promise me you won't bring it up!" Olivia said.

"Whatever, O," Lauren said. "I still can't believe Joel sent you roses. I knew he was always a bit sweet on you, but that seems like a little much, even for him."

"Crazy, huh?" Olivia said. "I don't think it means anything."

"Now you're being crazy. No man sends a girl red roses as a sign of friendship."

Lauren was correct, of course, which made Olivia's subterfuge all the more unbelievable. But Lauren's assessment also caused a pleasant stir deep inside of her again; Andrew wanted *her*.

* * *

They both finished up their shift and returned back to their apartment, but Lauren wasn't staying long; she had a hot date with Chris. The situation was a bit disconcerting as Olivia was alone this time. Usually they ended up double-dating or bar hopping with the current crop of lieutenants. This was the first time that Olivia wasn't attached. Lauren's seeming lack of concern that Olivia was being left behind made her a little resentful, but she was so caught up with excitement about her impending date that it was hard to be angry with her.

Lauren even asked her three-times if she looked all right, which was very odd behavior for her, considering her—well really their—track record with the lieutenants. She had gone the extra mile to look great. She wore a sleeveless cream dress, with black accents around the neck, which she paired with a pair of shiny black pumps. Olivia could have never gotten away with wearing that color without looking like a corpse. On Lauren, though, the combination made her olive skin looked warm and inviting.

"You really like him, don't you?" Olivia asked her.

Lauren blushed and then talked around the question. "He's sweet and old-fashioned. I just don't want to embarrass myself."

"Where are you guys going?"

"The Frigate," Lauren answered, nonchalantly.

Of course, it was the most posh seafood restaurant in the city. They didn't list prices on the menu, which was designed each week by the head chef the Frigate had poached from another restaurant in Manhattan. If Olivia remembered right, it only served a five-course meal for dinner. She didn't even know if they served lunch. One thing she did know was, set on pylons overlooking the bay; the view and atmosphere couldn't be more idyllic.

Olivia raised an eyebrow at her.

"What? It was his idea," Lauren said, defending herself. "I think it's pretty romantic."

"You'll have to tell me all about it later," Olivia said, but her tone didn't come out very cheerful.

"Oh, don't pull a 'poor O' on me," Lauren said.

"I'm sorry, I didn't mean sound sour." Olivia put on a happy face for Lauren's benefit.

"Oh, now you're making me feel guilty," Lauren said, seeing through it. "I tell you what. I'll get Chris to hook you up with one of his mates. We can double. Why don't you give Justin another chance? He seems interested—with the flowers and all."

"Definitely *not* Justin," Olivia said, remembering the awful encounter with him. "I really didn't mean to sound like a snot. Go have fun. You don't have to match me with anyone."

"Of course, there's always Joel." Lauren was smirking at her.

Olivia threatened to throw a pillow at Lauren, who only laughed at her. A horn honked outside.

"That's my ride," Lauren said.

Lauren grabbed her things and let herself out.

And then Olivia was alone.

She changed into sweats, made herself a grilled cheese, and settled in front of the TV, and settled down for a relaxing night in.. But there was nothing on she found even remotely interesting after cycling through the guide several times. She thought she might read, but gave up after rereading the same paragraph five times. Her focus was shot. Perhaps she should go out?

But Olivia couldn't think of where to go that wouldn't just be burning gas or time. She didn't want to go to a bar alone. She wasn't really interested in shopping, nor was it in her budget anyway. It was also getting too dark out to run, not that she would have anyway.

She was bored.

Worse, she had the fidgets, which meant she kept getting up, pacing aimlessly and then sitting down.

Her attention kept returning to her phone, which sat on the coffee table in front of her. She kept looking at it as if she might have missed a call, but it wasn't a missed call that was worrying at her; she knew she was resisting *making* a call; a call to a certain off-limits man that she wouldn't name. Of course, as soon as she denied herself the name, "Andrew" promptly popped into her head.

She didn't dare touch the device, but its siren call to her was insanely tempting her.

She got up and went back in the kitchen. Andrew's bouquet of roses was on the counter.

She couldn't see to get away from him.

Maybe she could call him to tell him she had received his flowers, but that they really couldn't see each other anymore? He would want to know she had received them, and she wanted him to know how much they meant to her, but they couldn't see each other again; that it couldn't work between them. Hospital rules, ethics rules, oaths and such—she played with the conversation in her mind, imagining that Andrew would accept the bad news as well as Tyler had. She was the roadblock, though. She was not reacting well to formulating the words; she really didn't want to say them.

She left the kitchen and retreated to her bedroom.

She tidied it up, not that it needed much cleaning, but it tended to get cluttered after a while with clothes she had tried on and discarded and other things she'd taken out and hadn't immediately put away. She even made the bed.

And then paired off all the loose socks in her drawers. She was pleased to find there were no stragglers; every sock had its mate, which made her feel even more stupidly alone.

Overall, it took her . . . fifteen minutes to clean.

The clock on her nightstand read 7:23 PM.

Ugh.

She needed to occupy herself with something or she was going to go insane. A quick check of her laundry revealed it wasn't full enough to spend precious quarters on yet. A brief thought of combining Lauren's stuff with hers flashed through her head, but was quickly dismissed. The last time she had combined loads, Lauren had gone apeshit over her choice of detergents.

She went back to the kitchen and moved the roses out of view, while she attacked the four or so dishes that had accumulated in the sink. Then she dried them and put them away.

All of which consumed another eight or so minutes . . .

She dusted off the television and restacked books and DVDs that had accumulated in the living room. She even reorganized them on the shelves . . . alphabetically.

Even then, the clock barely budged.

She was driving herself nuts and running out of busywork to keep her occupied. As it was, she was going to have to mess things up again or Lauren would clearly suspect she had become unhinged.

But there was only one way to scratch the itch she had.

Steeling herself, she marched back into the living room and grabbed her phone. She dialed Andrew's number, surprisingly, from memory. When she had memorized it, she wasn't sure.

It rang twice before he answered.

"Hello." Andrew's gravelly voice sent a shiver up Olivia's spine. Her knees even buckled.

She sat down on the couch, before they quit on her along with her resolve.

"Hi, it's Olivia."

Chapter 10

Olivia woke nuzzled in Andrew's arms, her cheek resting on his chest. Sunlight, streaming in through the French doors to the deck, had crept up on her. Drawn in through the windows, the salty sea breeze swirled in the bedroom, raising goose pimples on her exposed skin. Besides being wrapped in Andrew, she couldn't think of a more pleasant way to be awoken. The combination of the three was downright intoxicating.

Their phone call last night had lasted ten seconds. Once she identified herself he merely said "Come over." She had hung up and obeyed as fast as she could, not even bothering to change into regular clothes. In fact, it only just occurred to her that she hadn't even packed a bag. She couldn't get to his house fast enough.

It was as if she had been under some sort of all-consuming compulsion, which was completely alien to her.

Once there, he had commandeered her body and relentlessly worked her until she was a spent rag, wrung free of every drip of pleasure he could free from her. In some respects, she felt like she hadn't reciprocated enough, but he had assured her repeatedly he had what he needed from her—which, even though he left it unsaid, she knew was *control*.

She looked up at Andrew. He was still asleep, looking peaceful and content. She didn't want to move, but the call of nature was urging her out of bed.

Carefully, she tried to slide out from under his embrace. Her movement caused him to stir, though, and his eyes popped open.

"Good morning," Andrew said, smiling at her.

"Morning," she responded.

"Sneaking off, again?" Andrew feigned looking hurt.

Olivia knew he was playing, but she couldn't help thinking about when she had stormed out of his room at the hospital. Then, she had been—still was in reality—concerned about getting caught having an affair with a patient. It wasn't the same now that he was discharged, although she was sure Dr. Heriberto would have something to say about her new-found fling if he got wind of it. All the same, she felt rebuked.

She tried to not let her feelings show; he didn't understand her profession.

"Bathroom," she said, excusing herself.

She stepped to the bathroom adjoining his bedroom and shut the door behind her. Completing her business, she washed her hands and splashed some water on her face. An electric razor, stick of deodorant, toothbrush, toothpaste, hairbrush and a bar of soap were the only toiletries on the vanity top. He was so not a girl, she thought, smiling to herself.

To the back of the vanity, against the backsplash, almost hidden by the mirror and sink, a picture frame was lying on its face. Curious, Olivia picked it up and turned it around.

Andrew stood with his arm around the woman Olivia had had the run-in with, but Olivia's hackles weren't raised over that. No, it was the cute, little, toddler girl held snug between them that she couldn't peel her eyes from.

They looked so happy . . . the perfect *family*.

Olivia wanted to throw up.

She put the picture hastily back in its place and focused on calming her racing heart. Lots of people had relationships and failed marriages at some point in their lives. Some even had children. Why wasn't it possible that Andrew was one of those people—and why did it bother her? It wasn't like he had lied to her. Their prior relationships never came up. She'd had ample opportunity to ask, assuming she could have got a word in edgewise between their lovemaking sessions.

She was acquainted with his ex that had dumped the Frappuccino in her car seat. Were they just separated? Was she just a rebound girl that Andrew would discard once he found something better? Who had custody of the child? Did he even visit the little girl? Was he in arrears in child support?

She didn't know Andrew at all.

Her mind was racing with questions, some of which she had no right to ask. The more she thought about them, the more she wanted to escape back to her apartment.

She splashed some more water on her face and took a deep breath.

She stepped back into his room.

Andrew had gotten out of bed. Through the open French doors, she saw him standing on the deck, leaning on the railing and looking out to sea. He hadn't bothered to put on any clothes, which made her self-conscious for him. Why, she didn't know, because he looked amazing, with his sculpted back and shoulders that tapered down to strong hips and perfect ass. He had tied his long hair back up in a ponytail, which swished over the top of his upper back as he surveyed the ocean.

The scars on his left calf were made more visible by the shadows cast by the cratered skin in the morning sun.

The little self-consciousness she felt at stepping out onto the deck with Andrew was overridden by her desire to touch him.

Who was he and why did she want him so much?

As if sensing her presence, Andrew looked over his shoulder back at her. His serious expression softened into a smile and he beckoned her to him.

She joined him and he wrapped a strong arm around her and snugged her to his side. The heat of his body beat back the cool ocean breeze.

"Great view," she said.

"It is, isn't it," he said, as if he were noticing it for the first time.

"I guess it must get boring after awhile." Olivia knew she was being a bit flip, but his reaction puzzled her. She didn't understand how anyone could take this for granted. Most people, like her, only got to wake up to such a view while on a vacation in a hotel. He woke up to this every day.

Andrew looked at the bay, studying it. "No, it never gets boring. I come out here to think. It clears my head. Sometimes. Other times, not so much. I bought this land a couple of years ago. I even built this house." Andrew said looking around, admiring the property. "Pissed off my neighbor when he saw the plan. Sued me to stop construction because so a small place devalued his lot. He wanted me to build a mansion." Andrew looked at her and smiled again.

"Obviously you won?" Olivia asked.

"No, we settled. I doubled the size of the house and added the garage. Then I leased the back lawn as a vineyard to Newport Winery."

Olivia looked down at the sprawling plantation of grapes stretching to the Atlantic.

"Why?"

"I didn't want a protracted fight. Making it a bit bigger than the original plan was a small concession. The grapes sealed the deal. Amanda wanted a bigger house anyway. I just wanted the view. Everyone got what they wanted."

"Your ex-wife?" Olivia asked nervously.

"Ex-girlfriend. We never married."

She couldn't quite put her finger on whether Andrew sounded regretful or wistful, but she wasn't reassured by the sound of it either. Was Andrew devastated by an ugly breakup with Amanda? Was it enough to drive him over the edge? And what about the child?

The questions raced through her head even though she knew she couldn't pressure him for answers. She'd jumped head-first into the pool and didn't have a right to be surprised when she struck the bottom. The lure of the water had been too irresistible for her to overcome, and now she was stuck with the consequences of a broken neck.

She shook the line of thought from her head. She was being ridiculously melodramatic. If she never saw Andrew again after today, her life would be fine. She would go back to normal, chasing Navy guys with Lauren . . . and still feeling unsettled.

"You okay? You're pretty quiet." Andrew was looking down at her. Concern etched his eyes and his mouth had drawn into thin questioning smile. "It really is over. I don't see her anymore," he added, trying to reassure her. "She's in the past."

Olivia smiled back up at him, letting him know she understood even if she wasn't quite settled herself. It solved one bit of the puzzle, but left many unanswered questions that gnawed at her still. If the relationship were over, it was very recent. Recalling her run-in with her, Amanda still came to the house unannounced and was a possessive type. Even if Andrew thought it was over, she doubted Amanda would agree with him.

Such a possessive woman wasn't shaken so easily.

And having experienced Andrew up close and personal herself, she doubted that even she would release him easily or without a fight. Just thinking about him touching Amanda raised her hackles even though she didn't have any true claim on Andrew . . . yet.

She was so getting ahead of herself. And why he even elicited these feelings of wanting permanency was a mystery to her. Was he just the first man she decided to cling to? Some sort of strange rebound after Tyler and getting sick of bouncing between Navy classes? Or was it *him* that these feelings sprung from? She couldn't decide if her true feelings were eluding or deluding her.

Andrew leaned in and kissed her. The warm kiss and tickling of his stubble rekindled an ember in her gut for him. His kiss grew more vigorous, but she wasn't going to let him distract her so easily from the questions that burned within her. Her will was weakening, though, and she felt the bed behind her beckoning.

"And your daughter?" she asked, finally working up the nerve.

Andrew's face fell and turned stony. The warmth she felt from him was sucked away out to sea. His eyes grew cold and piercing. The transformation was sudden and complete. He looked away from her, back out into the bay. He didn't speak.

Her anxiety grew.

Her nerve faltered. "I'm sorry. It's none of my business," Olivia apologized.

Andrew still didn't say a word. He was gripping the railing so hard his knuckles were white. A tear beaded at his eye. He wiped it away quickly, resuming his iron grip of the railing.

"She died," he said. The words came out short and clipped.

Olivia's stomach reeled at the revelation. She was a shitbag. Here Andrew was in deep pain and she was consumed with petty jealousies.

She wanted to say something, but now she was speechless.

Fortunately, Andrew found his voice again, saying, "It was a year ago. She was four. She would be five now."

* * *

Andrew looked at Olivia. She hugged herself, looking shaken. Her lips quivered, trying to hold back a cry. He knew how she felt. He had the urge to roll her up in his arms and comfort her, but he knew if he did he wouldn't finish the story. He held fast to the balcony, afraid if he let go that he would change course and dive back into the warm safety of Olivia's embrace.

"We were riding our bikes together. She still had her training wheels on," he said, taking each sentence one at a time. "I had put on her helmet. I even wore one myself so she would think big people had to wear them, too."

Tears slipped from Olivia's eyes and down her cheeks. He desperately wanted to wipe them away, but he held onto the railing as if he might fall if he let his concentration lapse even for a moment.

"We were on the bike path. It should have been safe. Rollerbladers, other bicyclists, to look out for, but otherwise safe . . . ," He looked back out into the bay. "Even bike paths cross streets now and then," he said.

Andrew could feel the damn of tears building at his own eyes now.

"I tried to head her off, but she got away from me." His voice cracked at the end.

Andrew thought about stopping there, but he knew he had to go on and complete the story as Heriberto had instructed him.

"The truck," Andrew said, pausing as his chest fought to stifle him. He overpowered the urge to stop and continued, "The truck that hit her, it didn't kill her. The paramedics got there fast. They scooped her up, bicycle and all, and raced to the Children's Hospital. I hopped in the back of ambulance. Left my bike at the side of the road.

"She was awake . . .

"Alert . . .

"I held her hand."

Andrew took a deep breath, but continued, "She told me she would never race ahead again. I told her it was okay, and I loved her anyway. She just needed to get better now.

"But she didn't. She got some infection in the hospital. They couldn't control it. Five days later, it took her."

Olivia clutched herself for dear life, not unlike the way he was holding onto the railing. Her face was tear-streaked. She hadn't interrupted him.

Part of him wished she had.

Reliving the story was the worst pain he could put himself through. Every time he told the story it made Tia's death just that much more permanent, as if she were going to pop back to life one day if he denied it long enough.

"What was her name?" Olivia meekly asked.

"Christina," Andrew said, "Amanda called her 'Tina.'" Andrew smiled at the memory. "But she couldn't pronounce the 'n' when she was a toddler. She was my 'Tia.'"

He turned around to face Olivia and reached out his hands to her. She clasped them, with trembling hands.

"Tia's death broke something in me," Andrew said, trying to explain himself.

"She was your child," Olivia said. He saw the compassion and understanding in her face, her eyes. "I don't think any parent gets over that."

So he was learning; the hard way as usual, Kristen might say.

Of course, his denial over the past year was obvious to him now, but not then, not until his brush with his own death did he realize how bad a shape he was in. He had shut himself off from everyone and gone silently insane. Even work couldn't save him.

What little support he had, he had rejected. His relationship with Amanda already sucked, only Tia had held it together, and without her it had gone steadily downhill. Kristen was sympathetic—she was his sister; she had to be to some extent—but there was too much baggage between them. He was friendly with the cutting crews, but guys didn't talk about things like this.

"Thanks," Andrew said, pulling Olivia closer to him. He wrapped his arms around her and squeezed her against him. She squeezed him back.

"Thanks, for letting me in," Olivia said.

She rested her head on his chest. The rising sun warmed his back, as the sea breeze fought to cool him off. Elemental forces dueled at his back, but he was looking forward now. For the first time, there was hope, life looked manageable, and the future might include some happiness for him.

Chapter 11

Kristen paced in front of Andrew nervously. She was dressed in a suit, or what he assumed passed for a suit for women; a rare occurrence for her. The fact that she didn't have to wear a tie made him jealous. It was a damn noose, he thought, as he tugged at his collar with a finger.

"Quit your pacing, you're making me nervous," he said, finally.

Kristen scowled and mouthed *fuck off* in his direction.

They sat in a waiting area, alone, outside a conference room of National Power's offices. Although the sealed bids would be handled by the lawyers, Sid Biery, the regional vice president, wanted to see presentations from all the bidders. Sid's staff had sent invitations and scheduled private appointments for all the known bidders.

So here they were.

Normally, he would have left Kristen behind. He relented after her incessant pestering and the fact that she had brought this project to his attention when, to put it mildly, he wasn't in the best state of mind. He was beginning to regret letting her come, but he couldn't take that back now. And he knew, to a certain extent, that he needed to let her come. As much of a pain in the ass she could be, she would never get the hang of these meetings if he left her at the office all the time.

"What's taking them so long?' Kristen said. She had stopped pacing in front of him. She took a moment to smooth her skirt before sitting next to him on the bench.

"Sid always makes people wait," Andrew answered her.

"Douchebag."

"Yes, but a very important douchebag. One that could break us anytime he felt like it," Andrew warned.

"I know."

Andrew looked over at her. "You behave and control that mouth of yours," he said.

"Fuck you. I'm not a child."

"Then act like a woman and cut the language. Sid is old school."

"What's that mean?"

"If he asks you to get a cup of coffee, go get it," Andrew said.

Kristen looked back at him slack-jawed. "I don't have to put up with that shit," she said after regaining her composure.

"*This* is why I didn't want you to come." Andrew sighed.

"This is the fucking twentieth century," Kristen complained.

"Twenty-first," Andrew corrected.

"Fuck you."

"At least I know what century it is. And I don't care how bad he is, if he dropped us we would be ruined."

"We'd sue his ass."

"And what in the meantime? We would have to lay off half the crew. Sell the equipment. A lawsuit would take years—and we could lose." He could see the frustration spreading over her face. "Just do everyone a favor, please, and swallow that pride for once. That, or leave now. I should have listened to my gut and left you at home."

Kristen looked sullen. Her usual retort didn't even look poised on her lips.

"You're actually scared," Andrew said.

Kristen nodded.

Andrew knew that must have cost her to admit that to him, of all people.

"You'll be fine," he said, trying to reassure her. Despite their difficulties, she still was and always would be his sister.

She slumped, propping her chin with arm braced against a knee and nibbled on a finger.

After some silence she said, "What if I'm not?"

"Don't be defeatist."

Taking a break from her finger, she gave him a sour look.

"What's made you all 'Mr. Fucking Positive'?" she demanded.

He only smiled back at her, making her scowl.

And, no doubt about it, he had been chipper. Since his suicidal episode, he had been putting his life back together; no small part of which he owed to Olivia, who had somehow injected him with renewed hope that life was worth sticking around for a bit longer. And he found he didn't mind his counseling sessions; something Olivia had been very supportive of.

Even Amanda had seemed to take the hint—finally. He hadn't heard from her in weeks. He hoped it was the last, but fully expected she would interject herself again into his life when he least needed the interruption. He didn't need her coming around and dragging him into the past. The past was too painful, and if he could pretend it all never happened the better. He would obliterate the past by refusing to acknowledge it ever existed.

He had finally cleaned out the house of every last vestige of his former life, giving away his old furniture to Kristen and, what she didn't want, he gave to friends or guys from the crew. What he couldn't give or throw away went in storage. He had hired a decorator to paint and refurnish the place, completely making it over. Amanda would have been aghast if she had seen what he had done to the house, which brought a quirk of a smile to his lips just thinking about it. The stately, ornate, stodgy elegance of the house had been remade in contemporary style. He even replaced the light fixtures and blew out the wall between the dining room and study, opening the place up.

Not everything had gone, though. Even with his new outlook on life, Andrew couldn't bring himself to touch Tia's room. He'd left it as-is, but he'd also locked the door and put the key in the safe at the office. He wouldn't be tempted to wander in and rock in the rocking chair and brood. How many nights had he whiled away rocking in that chair? How many times had he read bedtime stories out loud to an empty bed? He didn't know, couldn't remember. But it wouldn't happen anymore.

The past was the past.

Now there was only Olivia. She had re-lit that spark, that ember, inside him that was the motivation to do something, anything. But it was fragile, like kindling that had barely caught. He was desperately afraid that the slightest breeze would snuff it out, and then he would be back where he was, without hope, without purpose.

"Ready?" Kristen said, bringing him out of his ruminations.

He nodded and stood, brushing his trousers flat and straightening his jacket. Good as new. If only fixing the rest of him were so easy.

"Let's go," He said.

The assistant escorted them into Sid's office. Sid was perched behind an L-shaped mahogany desk, scribbling away on a pad. The sunlight streaming in behind him was blinding; positioning Sid had undoubtedly set up on purpose to psychologically dominate his visitors. It was hard to negotiate with someone when you couldn't read their face without shading your eyes.

Sid stood up. Even with the sunlight and Sid's fake-bake tan, Andrew could see his whitened smile. Sid was fit, but had to be rapidly approaching fifty. All the eye and chin tucks in the world couldn't hold back the wheel of time forever. His hair had gone white ages ago, but was still thick, and with his height and pampered appearance, he looked rather distinguished.

"Andy, great to see you again," Sid said. Sid shook his hand vigorously, but wasn't a crusher like some.

"Great to see you too," Andrew said. "My sister, Kristen. Finance chief."

"Pleasure to meet the gal with the bucks," Sid said. "Why do you keep her locked up in the back office? You've gotta get this girl out more, Andy."

Sid took Kristen's hand gently and held it for an unnaturally long time, making Andrew tense. Andrew wasn't sure how much Kristen was going to tolerate before she put Sid in his place.

To Andrew's surprise, Kristen placed a hand over Sid's and said, "It's a pleasure to meet you too, sir. Andy gets a little overprotective of his little sister."

Sid whooped and placed his other hand over Kristen's and they kept shaking. Andrew's jaw might have hit the proverbial floor if his anger hadn't already reeled it in tight against his upper choppers. "Call me Sid, Kris. I can call you Kris, right?" Sid said and then, before Kristen could answer, added, "I'd be overprotective, too, if I had a sister as pretty as you."

"Oh, Sid!" Kristen said, chuckling and looking bashful.

Andrew couldn't quite decide whether he wanted to throw up or drag out of Sid's office Kristen by her hair. Neither looked like a great choice, but Kristen was hamming this up way too much. If he had been closer to her, he would have left a bruise on her leg by now with a knock-it-off kick.

"Well let's get down to business, shouldn't we?" Andrew suggested.

"Plenty of time for that," Sid said. He hadn't released Kristen's hands yet.

"Andy always was a kill-joy," Kristen said and they chuckled together like they had some sort of inside joke.

Andrew clenched his fists, and put on a strained smile. Kristen's chuckle deepened and her eyes smiled back at him at his obvious discomfort. Sid whooped again.

"I like you," Sid said, releasing Kristen's hands, finally. Sid took his seat again, signaling that it was appropriate for Kristen and Andrew to sit now as well.

* * *

Andrew didn't know what quite happened, but things had either taken a remarkable turn for the better or this was going to be an outright disaster for the firm. He should have left Kristen at the office.

He nearly broke the door off its hinges when he stormed back into the office alone, sending everyone scurrying for cover; afraid they were next. He apologized to no one in particular and retreated to his office in shame, closing the door so he didn't have to look at any of his petrified staff.

What was supposed to be a simple presentation had somehow turned into 'twenty questions with Kristen.' The flirting had been innocuous at first, but before he knew it, Sid had ended the presentation and invited Kristen for drinks on his yacht. Andrew had politely declined—but he hadn't been invited, either.

It was an unmitigated disaster.

The development caught him completely off-guard; worse, there was nothing he could do about it. And Kristen, being Kristen, didn't pass on the male attention, which arguably was coming from one of the richest and most powerful assholes on this side of the bay. She probably thought she was helping out the firm by humoring him, the stupid bitch. What did she think was going to happen to the firm if things didn't work out between the two of them? But she never thought things through before jumping in with both feet, which was why dad left him in charge in the first place.

He punched the wall in frustration, but the pain in his knuckles made him instantly regret it. He needed a padded office, the thought of which made him grin. He probably belonged in a padded *room*.

He tried to bury himself in reports and financials to cleanse his mind of the situation and chew through time. It was partially successful; when he finally looked up, the clock read six p.m. But it wasn't working anymore—he needed to get out of here. There was nothing more to be done and his mind was too wound to review reports and quotes anymore;

he caught himself re-reading the same paragraph five times now.

He scanned his phone for messages, but nothing from Olivia, which wasn't surprising. She had a swing shift this week and would be working until midnight, assuming her relief came in on time. There was nothing to do, but kill time and wait for her. He thought about taking some files home, but instantly dismissed the idea. He needed some distance from work now.

Perhaps he could persuade her to meet him at the Orchid after her shift ended at eight? Hell, he could get a head start there himself. He sent her a text and grabbed the truck keys.

* * *

Andrew took a seat at the bar. He ordered a boilermaker and a burger, but otherwise ignored everyone around him, including the noisy sailors occupying two of the back tables and the dipshit bartender's attempts to make conversation about "having a rough day?" at his drink choice—as if people hadn't gotten drunk in this place before.

The food came quickly, reminding him he hadn't eaten anything since lunch—he was starving. He scarfed the burger, ignored the soggy fries and, after messily dropping the shot of whiskey in the glass, depth charge-style, slammed the beer. He forgot how greasy the food here was.

He hailed the bartender and ordered another boilermaker.

He didn't really get how this place was one of Olivia's favorites, but knowing the bar's reputation, knew it wasn't the food that attracted people to it. The only reason he even knew she came here was because he had overheard her talking to a friend on her cell. He hadn't been to the Orchid in years, but it hadn't changed; or if it had, Andrew couldn't tell the difference. It was one of those bars that led a dual-life, sedate during the day, selling sandwiches to tourists walking the boulevard, and a party bar at night, thriving off of inebriated coeds and sailors. It was a shitty bar for a local, like him.

He ordered another boilermaker.

The bartender switched the TVs one at a time to the Red Sox game; even turning up the sound so everyone could hear the play-by-play. The announcers were chatting up their usual nonsense before the opening.

"Quite a season, huh?" the bartender said.

Andrew shrugged, and said, "I haven't been watching much."

He hadn't paid any attention to a game since . . . he shoved the memory back down, but it was too late; Tia's name blazed to the forefront of his brain, threatening to swallow everything in a wave of uncontrollable grief. He choked back the cry, masking it with a coughing fit.

"You okay, buddy?" the bartender asked, handing Andrew a napkin. "Wrong pipe?"

Andrew wiped his mouth and attempted to calm himself; counting backwards, counting forwards, reciting the alphabet silently to himself, tricks to defuse the rising wave of anxiety soaked grief.

"Here, have a glass of water." The bartender pushed a glass to him.

Andrew pushed it back, gulping down the rest of his beer instead.

"Well, that's one way to wash it out," the bartender said, laughing.

Andrew pulled his wallet out, counted out several bills and slapped them down to pay the tab. He needed to get out of here. He was falling apart and needed to find someplace to pull it back together.

The bartender looked at him sideways. "Everything okay, buddy?"

Andrew smiled weakly and got up, waving the bartender off. He turned to leave and, out of the corner of his eye, caught a girl staring at him. She was sitting with the sailors in the back. On the lap of one, in fact. She had a vaguely familiar face, but he couldn't remember where he'd met her before. It didn't matter . . . she didn't matter . . . nothing mattered. He needed to get out of this place; it was suffocating him.

Chapter 12

Olivia hustled down to the Orchid. Andrew's text had caught her off guard, as unusually blunt as it was. Something must have been off, but what she didn't know. Andrew didn't much like going out, which had suited her fine. The more time she could put between his trip to the hospital and her work there the more attenuated any accusation of an "unprofessional relationship" became. It had been several weeks now, but she still grew paranoid at the thought someone at the hospital would find out and file a complaint with the director or, god forbid, the licensing board. But even that fear hadn't been enough to keep her from returning to Andrew. She hadn't felt so content with a man in . . . , well . . . , never. She had seen him at his worst and, she liked to believe, helped nurture him back to health. His psyche had been so fragile back then—as if years had passed, not weeks—but now was infused with strength and an incredible work ethic. He threw himself into everything, 100%, sometimes, much to her dismay when he would call her to cancel a date. As disappointed as she was when that occurred, it didn't happen often, and it was hard to be too upset when she knew he had a business to run.

She hadn't moved in with him. She couldn't leave Lauren hanging with the lease, and as comfortable as she felt with Andrew, she didn't want to throw in with him until she knew this relationship had legs; at least a little more time under her belt . . . *and up her skirt and under her shirt*, she added to the thought wryly. He had pestered her a couple of times to move in; even going so far as remodeling the damn house and replacing the bedframe and mattress—talk about excessive. He probably would have held a ceremonial bonfire for the old mattress if she had demanded it, which brought a warm glow inside her chest.

In any case, she might as well have moved in considering the amount of time she spent there. Lauren wasn't too suspicious because she was spending all her nights at Chris's dorm in base housing, but she was starting to nag a bit that Olivia wasn't coming out with them enough. There were lots of cute Navy guys, she would say, trying to cajole Olivia into joining them at whatever bar they decided to go to that night. Worse, she kept trying to match her up with Justin. Olivia didn't mind giving people second chances, but Justin didn't deserve a second chance and she didn't have any interest anyway. Andrew was her world now.

Olivia walked into the Orchid and glanced around, looking for Andrew. He'd said he was seated at the bar, but no one had his distinctive back and broad shoulders. Joel was working the bar and gave her a little wave, which she returned with a smile.

She walked to bar. "Make me a Cosmo?" she asked him. She needed something strong and fruity.

Joel nodded and set to work, mixing her drink. "Just get off?" he asked.

"Yeah," Olivia said, scanning both up and down the bar just to make sure she hadn't somehow missed Andrew. Perhaps he was at the rear bar, she thought, but a quick look confirmed he wasn't there; and the vacant barstools told her no one else was either. Her stomach tightened at spotting Lauren and Chris and the rest of his crew stationed at two back tables. She hadn't expected seeing them here, but where else would they have gone? She knew she should have persuaded Andrew to go somewhere else, but all she had was Andrew's abrupt text and she hadn't given it much further thought.

Lauren spotted her and looked a little irritated. Olivia fought the reflex to look away, and put on a fake smile.

"Here you are." Joel handed Olivia her drink. She paid him and collected the cosmo. She took a sip, collecting herself before walking over to Lauren.

Lauren was perched on Chris's lap. Chris had a hand up her miniskirt, but Lauren seemed oblivious. Looking more closely at her face, Olivia saw the telltale glaze over Lauren's eyes; she was smashed. Lauren's irritated look from earlier was since replaced with a smug smile. What she could be smug about, Olivia had no idea. Lauren could be such a bitchy drunk sometimes.

"Thought you said you couldn't come?" Lauren asked, huffily, as if she had something to be put out about.

Olivia shrugged and smiled back. "Thought I'd swing by," she said. What else could she say; she was kind of trapped now. She was going to have to resort to a lame excuse to escape. *Was she tired or did she have a headache?* It didn't really matter; she needed to find out where Andrew was. She must have misread the text and he was actually hanging out in another bar right now, waiting for her and either worrying or angry at getting blown off. She double-checked her phone—no, he had texted the Orchid. So *where was he?*

Out of the corner of her eye, she saw Justin eyeing her. He was seated at the far side of the table—next to the only open seat, of course—nursing a beer. If she had to stay for a few minutes to keep up appearances, she certainly wasn't sitting there; better to remain standing, except for the fact that her feet were killing her from standing all day. She grabbed a chair from the adjacent table and dragged it close to Lauren and Chris.

"What's up? You look distracted," Chris asked, his brow furrowed.

His question brought Olivia out of her funk, at least a little anyway. And his concern brought a genuine smile to her face. Chris, surprisingly, had turned out to be a rather decent guy, running counter to Olivia and Lauren's more common experience of the lieutenants passing through, who were only interested in getting laid—not that Olivia or Lauren had wanted anything else either—but it was a nice change to see Lauren growing attached.

"Sorry . . . just fretting over probably nothing," Olivia said, trying to snap her attention back on the here and now.

"Oh, she's just too good to hang out with us anymore," Lauren said, slurring her words. Lauren shifted in Chris's lap, leaning closer to Olivia. Lauren's skirt was riding high; showing a bit more than Olivia really cared to see. Combined with Lauren's beer breath, Olivia's stomach was starting to churn. Was this how Olivia looked on their drunken nights on the prowl? She was embarrassed for Lauren. "Why don't you hang with me anymore?" Lauren asked, looking a bit weepy.

"Stop it now. You know that isn't true," Olivia said, but the truth was Lauren's complaint did have ring of truth to it. Since meeting Andrew, Olivia had grown distant from her old way of life. If she hadn't met Andrew, no doubt she would have been here with Lauren, probably attached to one of the other lieutenants. She looked around the table. Justin was still eyeing her, but looked away at being spotted. Hell, she might have even given Justin another chance. With only a three-month commitment, she might have considered it. He was the handsomest of the lot in this session's classes.

"It is too true. You haven't come out with us in weeks." Lauren pouted.

Olivia couldn't disagree, but she was tired of jerks and flings and lieutenants wanting her to give up everything to travel across the country and be a military wife. Olivia didn't want to move away or give up her career. Her place was here, and she was sick of men passing through that just wanted to play grab ass while they were in town.

"When is graduation?" Olivia asked Chris with a smile, but not bothering to wait for an answer, Olivia redirected her attention at Lauren. "How can we keep doing this? Aren't you sick of bouncing from guy to guy?" Lauren looked taken aback as Olivia's outburst. "I'm sick of the merry-go-round. I'm sick of having my heart broken or doing the breaking. I'm sorry . . . I don't want to do this anymore," Olivia said. She pushed her chair back and stood up.

Lauren's nerve returned and she bounced out of Chris's lap, leaning inches from Olivia's face. "When did you get so judgmental? I have fun. We're having fun, or we used to have fun," Lauren said, loudly. All eyes turned to them, but Lauren seemed oblivious. Chris tried to pull Lauren back down into his lap, but she slapped his hands away.

"I'm leaving," Olivia said. She didn't get three paces before Lauren grabbed her elbow..

"I'm not letting you go." Tears welled in Lauren's eyes and her lips trembled.

No longer able to snap at her, Olivia hugged Lauren instead. "This is stupid," Lauren said, blubbering. "No one died."

Olivia nodded and shushed Lauren quiet. "It's okay. I'm just in a different place right now. I haven't forgotten you." Olivia release Lauren from the embrace and looked at her face. Lauren seemed to understand. "I need to go. I have to find someone I thought was going to meet me here."

"You've got a new boyfriend." Lauren whispered, in realization.

"Yeah," Olivia said.

"He's special isn't he?"

"Yeah." Olivia even felt a little flutter in her chest in anticipation of seeking Andrew.

"Okay. I knew you were being secretive, but you've outdone yourself this time," Lauren said with some semblance of cheer returning to her demeanor. "And you're going to spill the details to me later," Lauren demanded.

Olivia smiled. The gig was up now she knew, but she still thought she deserved an award for how long she'd managed to keep her and Andrew's relationship secret. Lauren would have to be sworn to secrecy. The more time she could put between Andrew's admission to the hospital and the day the hospital management learned about the relationship, the more attenuated the ethical considerations became. And then, hopefully, nonexistent. She longed for the day Andrew and she wouldn't have to hide the relationship from her peers anymore.

"I will," Olivia said to Lauren. "But I need to go now." Lauren nodded, her cheer finally returned. Olivia wished she bounced back from upset as quickly as Lauren could, but she knew she tended to ruminate on things until her stomach cried 'uncle.'

Olivia stopped at the ladies' before leaving the Orchid. She called Andrew and sent him a text, but he didn't respond to either, making her worried. She supposed his phone could have run out of juice or that he might have left it in his truck, but he was usually fastidious about making sure he had that phone with him, fully charged, because running the family business consumed him most of the time. She decided to swing by the house. His invitation to go out had been unusual, there had to be some explanation. If he was anywhere it was either home or his office. She wouldn't know where else to look, since Andrew didn't seem to have a social life outside of her.

There's no reason to worry, she told herself. They had just got their wires crossed and he was likely sitting back at the house wondering where the hell she was.

She left the toilet and made her way to the front door only to find Justin had tailed her. Confused as to why he had followed her, she asked, "What do you want?"

"You should stay," Justin said. "I know I was an asshole, before, but you shouldn't hold it against Lauren."

"You don't know what you're talking about," Olivia snapped at him. She contained the urge to roll her eyes at him. "You're not anything to do with anything."

"What does that even mean?" he asked.

"You know what I mean," she said exasperated. "It's none of your business."

"Come on. You can't hold this against me forever," he pleaded. "You never even acknowledged the flowers."

"They were nice. Thank you," she said.

"Com on. They were more than just nice."

Olivia couldn't even remember now what the bouquet looked like, but she was sure it had been impressive. It didn't matter and Justin was beginning to be more than annoying now.

"I really can't remember them. I'm not interested."

"What's it take to get a fresh start from you? Doesn't anybody get a second chance?"

Olivia finally did roll her eyes. "Seriously, are you tone deaf? I don't care whether you're here or not. I've got a boyfriend." That seemed to get through to him, as his eyes widened a bit and his mouth made an 'O' in response.

Olivia left Justin in the vestibule and headed to the lot. Her sun-faded Miata chirped at her in response to her keying the unlock button on the fob. She climbed in, closing the door and buckling up, only to have the wits scared out of her by Justin knocking on her window.

She cracked open the window. "What?" she said through the opening. She added some extra crank to her tone, hopefully making her irritation entirely clear.

"I just wanted you to know I was sorry," he said.

"Apology accepted. It's all under the bridge," she said, tersely. "I've got to go."

He gave her a dumb look, but was still transfixed inches from her window.

"Can you move a wee bit so I can pull out without hitting you?" she asked, although maybe hitting him wouldn't be such a bad thing. She could rid herself of a problem and get a deep sense of satisfaction from it—except it would likely backfire on her, and he'd end up assigned to one of her beds where she would have to wipe his ass and give him sponge baths.

"Oh, yeah," he said, taking a step back. A stupid smile played across his mouth, making her want to slap him. Did he think she was flirting with him or something?

She started the car and pulled out. Looking the rearview mirror she saw Justin watching her leave. More irritation zinged up her spine. She hoped this was the last time she would see him. Some guys just never seemed to take a hint.

Her cup holder lit up. Someone had messaged her phone. It was Andrew.

Chapter 13

The message read *"jjjj89k"* torpedoing Olivia's sense of relief. The message was nonsensical; he must have pocket-dialed her, she thought. She headed to his house, driving as fast as she dared; the Rhode Island cops tended to be sticklers about the speed limit and she didn't need the hassle of being pulled over even if they let her go with only a warning.

She pulled into Andrew's driveway only to realize he probably wasn't home; everything was dark, except the outside lights. No light emanated from any of the windows. She circled the cul-de-sac and brought the car to a stop, but left the engine running. She fished her phone from the cup holder and dialed Andrew. The phone rang and rang, but there was no answer, until she was dumped into voicemail, where Andrew's cheery voice instructed her to leave a message. She tried to hide the irritation and worry from her voice as she left a message asking where he was. She even tried to take the blame for getting their wires crossed for some reason. She ended the call and sent him a text asking where he was, even omitting "the hell" from between the "where" and "r u?" in the text.

She didn't want to drive all around Newport looking for him, but she didn't want to wait in his house or go back to her apartment either. Had she gotten the time wrong? Had he sent her the wrong location? She couldn't think of where he would be . . . except perhaps his office. Maybe something had held him up from leaving? She didn't know the reason, but he was going to get an earful when she found him.

Medina Tree Service was on the other side of the island in Middletown. Olivia avoided downtown, cutting through the developments instead. It added to the length of her trip, but at least avoided the congestion.

Arriving finally at the office, she saw the lights were on inside. A convertible Mercedes was parked out front in the visitor's lot. She didn't see Andrew's truck, but he would have been parked out back, in the employee's lot. She parked next to the Mercedes and got out of her car, taking a moment to smooth her dress. Andrew must have had a client drop in unexpectedly or some other emergency that needed tending. She could forgive him that—once he apologized adequately for not responding to her calls and texts, and making her worry.

She stepped up the front steps and let herself in. She didn't announce herself in order to not interrupt them. She would just wait for them to finish up, before making herself known. Only half the lights were on in the office. Most of the offices with doors were dark. Indistinct voices wafted from the back.

She had met Andrew here a couple of times, before heading out to dinner, but otherwise hadn't really taken in the place before. It had the same impeccable craftsmanship as his house, with nothing too ornate, just classy.

She took a seat in one of the comfy chairs in the waiting area and scanned the selection of stale magazines, but nothing looked like a worthwhile read, even to pass the time here. She crossed her leg over her knee and sat back in the chair, letting her earlier irritation ebb away so she didn't come off looking like a sourpuss, control-freak when Andrew finally emerged from his office. She kicked her crossed leg lazily, when a high-pitched giggle grabbed her attention bringing her kicks to an immediate halt . . . a distinctly female giggle . . . a coy and playful giggle.

Olivia didn't have any reason to be jealous, but the feeling surged instinctually through her at the sound. She calmed herself and uncrossed her legs, sitting up a bit more. She even leaned a bit out of her seat toward where the giggle had come from. She knew she was trying to eavesdrop now, but she felt no shame. She was justified even. Andrew shouldn't have kept her waiting like this, she told herself.

Whatever conversation there had been had ended; she couldn't hear any voices.

Olivia exhaled when she found she was holding her breath. She was being silly. She should just go and knock. Perhaps Andrew needed rescuing from a meeting that had droned on and on, and he would be grateful that she interrupted them, she tried to convince herself.

She stood up and nervously smoothed her dress again.

She would just march up to his door and announce herself. That way he would have to deal with her then and end whatever late night meeting had stolen him from her.

She took two steps towards the back when she heard a low coo followed by a throaty moan.

Anger surged through her and before she realized it fully, she was marching stiff-legged to the lone, lit office in the back. As she neared the office, the rhythmic slapping of sex assaulted her ears, making the bile rise in her stomach. She refused to believe Andrew would be cheating on her, but she couldn't run away; she needed to know, she needed to see. Tears welled in her eyes as she choked back the cry that wanted to escape her lips.

"I'm coming," the woman's voice whispered, followed by a hoarse "me too," from the man.

Olivia stepped into the open office doorway and yelled, "stop!" her arm outstretched as if she were a traffic cop controlling the flow of traffic.

The couple on the desk lurched in surprise. The woman attempted to cover herself up, the man jerked away from her, pulling futilely for his pants that had slipped down around his ankles. Olivia's anger fizzled and turned to acute embarrassment as she realized Andrew wasn't there. The man she didn't recognize; but the woman was Kristen, Andrew's sister.

"Um . . . my mistake . . . thought you were someone else . . . carry on," Olivia said, humbly. She tried to tear her eyes from the scene, but found herself eerily transfixed by the oddity of Andrew's younger sister getting it on with a man that looked old enough to be her father.

"What the fuck?" Kristen demanded, while the man continued to fumble for his pants.

Olivia snorted then laughed. Clasping a hand to her mouth to keep from laughing too hard, she then turned and raced from the office Kristen's cursing chasing her all the way. She felt so foolish yet relieved that Andrew hadn't been there. Outside her Miata, Olivia fumbled for her keys and dropped them, she was laughing so hard. She bent down and hunted for them in the gravel driveway, the darkness making the search difficult. "Fuck," she cursed at her predicament between her laughs.

She found the keys just under the lee of the car door, where they would have been out of sight if she hadn't gotten down on her knees. She stood up and unlocked the door. Before Olivia could get in, Kristen came barreling out of the office.

"Wait!" Kristen cried, causing Olivia to hesitate. Kristen, mostly dressed now, ran over to her, still tucking and buttoning things as she spoke rapidly, "You can't tell Andrew," Kristen said.

Olivia, composed now from the earlier surprise, replied calmly, "It's okay. I'm the one that should be embarrassed."

Kristen continued to ramble over Olivia giving a number of excuses, making Olivia think she had just nabbed her daughter doing the nasty instead of an adult. "Really, Kristen, it's none of my business. I came by the office because I thought Andrew was here and then when I heard people in the back I snooped instead of announcing myself. It's not your fault," Olivia said, trying to calm Kristen. Olivia's words seemed to have an effect on Kristen, who became visibly calmer.

"I'm not sure who was more surprised, you, Sid, or me, when you came screaming around that corner," Kristen said with a chuckle. "Did you really believe Andrew was cheating on you?"

Olivia was glad for the dim light because she could sense her ears getting warm. "I might have thought something along those lines," she said, adding a sheepish smile.

"Hah! You've got nothing to worry about there. I've never seen him in better shape since," Kristen said, hesitating, "well, since, a year ago." Kristen shoveled the gravel with a toe. "Were you supposed to meet him here?"

"No, that's what's got me worried. He texted me earlier to meet at the Orchid, but he wasn't there when I arrived," Olivia explained. "He wasn't at his house either."

Kristen's smile drew tight and worry lines creased her eyes. "I'm not sure where he would be then," Kristen said, but Olivia got the sense that Kristen was lying to her.

Kristen didn't know about Andrew's accident, Olivia knew that, too. Andrew was very private, and had admonished Olivia to keep the episode from getting out to his

146

family. He had told her that he didn't want them to worry, but Olivia gathered his relationship with his sister was complex. She agreed so long as Andrew would go to counseling, a promise he had kept.

But this was the first time that Andrew had disappeared on her—and the longer he stayed out of contact, the deeper her worry grew. If Kristen knew where Andrew might be, it was important that she say so. The last thing Olivia wanted was to find out that Andrew had a crisis and relapsed in despair when she was in a position to help him.

"If you know where I could find him, you need to tell me," Olivia said.

"He gets in these moods sometimes. You can't force him to do anything," Kristen said. "He just needs to work it out himself."

"It's more than just a mood or some funk he can deal with," Olivia said. "Please tell me."

"You're so fucking dramatic. He's probably sitting at another bar, pissed you've blown him off," Kristen countered.

"Then why doesn't he answer his phone?" Olivia asked, showing Kristen Andrew's garbled text. Kristen shrugged. "I'm not being drama queen. Andrew hasn't been dealing with Tia's death well at all—he blames himself. He's so guilty about it he nearly offed himself," Olivia said. Kristen's eyes widened, but she still looked a little incredulous. At least Olivia had her attention now. "I met Andrew several weeks ago in the hospital; he nearly died from carbon monoxide poisoning."

Kristen's jaw had dropped open with Olivia's revelation. Olivia knew Andrew would be angry with her later, but it was important that she find Andrew now and she didn't have time to waste futzing around with Kristen.

Olivia could see the gears turning in Kristen's head as she contemplated the revelation. "That's why he disappeared those couple of days. That son-of-a-bitch never said a word," Kristen said. Kristen looked at the sky then the ground again. "You stupid jerk," Kristen said under her breath. Looking at Olivia, Kristen said, "There are two places I could see him going to tonight, if he was . . . dwelling on the accident. The scene . . . or Amanda's place," and then asked, "You don't think he'd try again do you?"

"I don't know. He was doing so well until tonight, but something must have set him off," Olivia said. "That, or I am being completely hysterical and his phone is just dead. He's never done this to me before. My gut tells me he's in trouble."

And Olivia's guts were in knots, tied uncomfortably in several different clumps. The knots or her worry and the knots she realized of her growing love for Andrew. She had seen him at his worst and it didn't matter; she loved him. She knew from the knots in her stomach, now in worry, to the ends of her fingers when she caressed him, to the trembling in her knees when he held her tight, lifting her to the tips of her toes so she could reach high enough to kiss him and look him in the eye.

And she believed he felt the same way about her. She had seen how he had patched himself back together ever so carefully, still protecting that weak, tender tear in his heart; the wound that only a parent that had lost a child could ever knew and that would never quite heal completely no matter how much attention was paid it. There was just no recovery from such a loss—just coping and doing the best you could and taking each new day with an inhaled breath that was held and held until it was slowly let out because the breath was spent.

Olivia thought Andrew had hit bottom and was finally bouncing back. Putting himself together with her help. But perhaps she was wrong. Perhaps it was a façade . Another one of his carefully-built walls designed to shield him from the pain rather than engaging it and defusing it as best one could. Panic crawled up Olivia's throat at the thought—as she suspected—that it was indeed the case that Andrew had only been partially healing, while whiling away at his internal wall. The renovations to the cliff house were a distraction, something he could throw himself into to distract him from the rest of the pain in his life.

Despair and doubt tore at Olivia's heart, too, as she realized that maybe she hadn't been enough for him. That maybe Andrew couldn't be happy even with her. She thought he had needed her as much as she him; but maybe even she was another distraction.

She wiped tears from her eyes. It couldn't be true. He had to love her as much as she loved him. He couldn't throw their love away. She had to find him one way or another. She had to make sure he was safe. Then they could deal with whatever their relationship was. Was she just a crutch or was there more between them? She refused to believe that he didn't love her, but the weevil of a thought had bored its way into her head laying its eggs along the way to sprout into parasitic creatures of doubt to gnaw at her senses.

Even if he didn't love her, she still loved him and needed to see him safe. Knowing that, she could end things if she had to, heartbroken again. It would be better for everyone. She wouldn't have to worry about getting fired anymore and Andrew could get the help he needed. She could then disappear from his life and return to her previous life. Maybe she just wasn't meant to fall in love and live happily ever after. At least Lauren would be happy to have her back to her old party ways again.

Having collected herself and girded her resolve, finally, Olivia knew what she needed to do. "Where did the accident occur and where can I find Amanda?" she asked.

Kristen gave Olivia directions and then added, "I'll call the police and tell them to be on the lookout for him, and then I'll help you look for him."

Chapter 14

Olivia drove to the bird sanctuary, along Hanging Rock Road. Kristen had told her the accident occurred along the bike path at one of the main crosswalks. The sanctuary wrapped around the land surrounding Second Beach, only the lots, roads and park buildings disrupting the otherwise undeveloped land. Ordinarily, Olivia would have been captivated by the moonlit view, but under the circumstances it was hard to find pleasure in the trip.

She drove slowly around the curves in the road. Kristen said there would be a white cross on the side of the road marking the location where Christina had died. Olivia spotted the cross as she rounded a bend, just like Kristen said, its white paint reflecting her headlights.

She pulled into a nearby lot and parked the Miata. Several other cars were parked in the lot as well. Olivia could make out the silhouettes of couples in some of the cars. Others no doubt taking an evening romantic stroll on the beach itself. She scanned the lot looking for Andrew's truck, but she didn't spot it among the other parked cars. Her heart ached; she needed to find him.

Not able to leave yet, Olivia got out of the car and walked to the memorial marker. The white cross was erected about four feet from the curb, facing oncoming traffic. "Christina Faith Medina" was engraved and painted black on the crosspiece, making it stand out from the stark white paint of the rest of the cross. A fresh bouquets of flower lay at the base, among several dead bouquets. Someone had been here today, but Olivia couldn't be sure it was Andrew; Amanda could have placed these or someone else; another family member or even a Samaritan.

Andrew simply wasn't here.

Olivia returned to the Miata and set out for Amanda's place. Kristen told her that since Andrew had broken up with her, Amanda had been living with her parents in Middletown, just north of the bird sanctuary. Her stomach was full of butterflies now, because she didn't trust how she would react if she saw Andrew's truck there. Olivia knew she would in some sense be relieved that he was safe, but seeing he actually went to his ex-girlfriend for whatever reason, and blew Olivia off, gnawed at her insides and created a knot of tension in the back of her head. She didn't want to be jealous, it seemed so . . . petty. If Andrew needed to talk to someone about his grief over Tia, who better than Amanda? But why not her? Didn't she deserve his trust now? Hadn't she earned it? Olivia was so conflicted.

Olivia slowed as she approached the address Kristen had given her. A row of arbor vitaes hid the driveway from view. Olivia slowed down, her intent to make sure she got a good look at the driveway for Andrew's truck. The dualie would be hard to miss, but she didn't want to blast past the house and miss it if it were concealed behind the trees. She glanced to the driveway as she rolled past, and her heart thudded in her chest as she spotted the tailgate and the unmistakable wheels.

Andrew *had* come to Amanda's and she was crushed. Logically, she wanted to tell herself that it didn't matter, but it did. She wanted Andrew to come running to her and he hadn't. It was just like Amanda had said to her weeks ago in their chance encounter—Andrew was connected to Amanda and Olivia didn't have a chance.

She felt so stupid.

Olivia gunned the accelerator, racing away from Amanda's house, but not able to escape the pain it caused her. Her face was wet from tears. She thought about pulling over and just having a good cry, but the compulsion to drive, to do something had seized control. She didn't want to go to her apartment—she needed someone to talk to before she had a mental collapse. She needed Lauren.

Her decision made, she headed back into downtown Newport and to the Orchid. She prayed that Lauren was still there and wasn't completely hammered, but a drunken Lauren was better than no Lauren and would do at this point. Olivia just needed a familiar face she could talk at for a little while and vent the pain out of her before it ate her insides out and possibly be talked down to reality that things were not as dire as they seemed.

Olivia's phone rang. She snatched it out of the cup holder. It was Kristen. "I found him at Amanda's," Olivia said, not bothering to greet Kristen. The silence started to get pregnant, eliciting a nervous laugh from Olivia. "He's okay. You can call off the search. I'm meeting friends at the Orchid, I've gotta go," she added, begging off the call before Kristen could drill her on specifics. Olivia knew she couldn't keep her voice from cracking if she had to dwell on reality right now, and Kristen surely didn't need a wheelbarrow full of Olivia's insecurities dumped on her.

The traffic was slow-going through America's Cup Drive, which was nothing unusual for this time of night. Tourists and coeds filled the sidewalks, dotted with clumps of sailors in their dress whites. Olivia scored and found some on-street parking not far from the Orchid. She would still have to hoof it there, but it wasn't far and better than if she had to drive up and down the side streets looking for a space she could safely take without pissing off an apartment dweller.

She grabbed her clutch and started walking. The cool night air and salty breeze was calming, and just putting some distance between Amanda's house and getting back on familiar turf had a placebo effect on her nerves. Andrew was fine, she was fine, they would meet up tomorrow and have a good laugh about how silly she had been to worry. Andrew would apologize to her and tell her some silly story, like he had dropped his phone in the bay and couldn't call her. They would laugh and then make love again, perhaps on the deck again overlooking the bay. Everything would be fucking great.

Olivia's eyes teared-up again. She wiped them away quickly with the back of her hand. She needed to get a handle on herself. She couldn't go into the Orchid and burst into uncontrollable tears. She tried to put on a happy face, but she the muscles in her face were so taut and strained at the attempt at smiling, she gave up.

The Orchid came into view and Olivia quickened her pace, which proved to be a mistake. Her right heel rolled on the uneven sidewalk, twisting her ankle hard. Hot pain shot up her leg. By some miracle she didn't go sprawling on the walk. A stranger steadied her and helped her to an empty spot on one of the benches lining the street.

"That looked like it hurt," the stranger said. "Are you sure you're going to be okay?"

Olivia thanked him and reassured him she would be fine. He left her on the bench, nursing her ankle. She slapped the bench as if it were to blame for her bad luck. Like she needed the universe piling on right now. She flexed and rotated her foot, testing the ligaments. She didn't think she'd sprained it, but it was very sore, probably a strain. She stood up and gently tested some weight on the ankle. It held, but she definitely wasn't dancing tonight. She looked back towards her car and wondered whether it might just be better to go home now.

Against the nagging voice in the back of her head, she decided to press on to the Orchid. She hadn't come all this way not to see Lauren ,and if her ankle throbbed tomorrow, so be it.

* * *

The glare of the headlights shining in his eyes startled Andrew awake. He woke confused and banged his head on the door pillar before realizing he was still in his truck. He glanced outside, trying to figure out where he was. The yellow colonial and BMW in front of him jarred his memory— somehow he had ended up in Amanda's driveway. He didn't know how he had gotten here or for how long he had been passed out. Somewhat amazingly, the truck was parked perfectly straight behind the BMW. Apparently, Amanda or her parents hadn't even noticed he was parked in their driveway; or if they had, they had left him there. Knowing Amanda that may have very well happened. He could imagine her bitching that he could stay in the truck all night until he was sober. She would have had a hell of time anyway trying to move him, even with her father's help.

The dash clock informed him it was almost midnight. He straightened his seat back and started the truck, but one glance at his phone paralyzed him. His phone had exploded with notifications for text and voice messages from both Olivia and Kristen.

Where R U?

Followed by,

Call me

Listening to the first message only deepened his worry and shame. He smacked the steering wheel in frustration. It didn't help.

"Hey, it's Olivia, just wondering where you are," Olivia's said in a first message, followed by another message thirty minutes later growing more agitated.

Shit, she was supposed to meet him at the Orchid and he had left without calling her. His head throbbed. A half-empty fifth of cinnamon schnapps sat in the passenger seat mocking him. He vaguely remembered picking it up at the packy after leaving the Orchid, and hazily swigging the crap as he wallowed in his self-pity after recovering somewhat from his earlier panic attack. His tolerance for alcohol had gone to shit since meeting Olivia, no doubt for the better.

The next message was worse.

"Hey, you stupid motherfucker," Kristen said in the voicemail, "you'd better let us know where you are. Olivia and I are worried sick about you. You'd better not do anything stupid. Call us."

Kristen . . . always so charming, he thought. But then he did a mental double take. He replayed the message. Why had she said, "You'd better not do anything stupid"? What the hell was going on?

He dialed Olivia. The phone rang three times. He cursed under his breath. She had to pick up. He didn't want to leave a message—not that he didn't deserve it if she were ignoring his call now. Instead of getting kicked to voicemail, someone answered the phone. "Hello," Olivia said. Andrew recognized her voice, but she sounded weary.

"I'm so sorry. I . . . ," Andrew started, but Olivia interrupted him.

"Why . . . Why'd you go to Amanda's?" she asked, her voice cracking. "Don't you love me?"

Andrew felt like a dog now and was confused. How did she know he was even here? "Where are you? I'll be right there."

"Stay. I'm so angry . . . and tired . . . and worried for nothing. I'm so stupid. You made me feel so stupid. I thought we had something." Olivia was pitched as she rambled.

"I didn't mean it. I didn't. I'm sorry," Andrew said, backpedaling. "Where are you?"

"I can't even look at you now," Olivia said. "Just leave me alone. My ankle is killing me and I can't even concentrate. I'm hanging up."

And she really did hang up on him.

Andrew looked at his phone in disbelief. What the fuck just happened?

He dialed Kristen, who picked up on the second ring. "Are you okay? Where the hell have you been?" she asked.

"Nowhere," Andrew responded, then asking, "What did you say to Olivia?"

"Nothing," Kristen said, "she came to me worried you were going to hang yourself or something." Andrew's gut tightened. He didn't know whether to be pissed that Olivia had revealed his weakness to Kristen or appreciative that she cared for him so deeply. "You aren't going to are you?" she asked, laughing nervously.

"No," Andrew answered.

"It's not your fault," Kristen said, but Andrew understood what she was driving at.

"I know," Andrew said, lying. Everyone told him that Tia's death wasn't his fault, but he didn't believe it. He was supposed to protect her. He had failed. She was dead. It *was* his fault.

Kristen saw through it, though, saying, "Quit being a tough guy. I left you alone 'cause I thought you needed the space, but that was my mistake. Lean on me. We're family. And you need to keep that Olivia. She cares about you."

"I think I may have fucked that up, too," Andrew said.

"You go and fix it, then," Kristen said, chastising him.

"She's pissed at me and she won't tell me where she is," he said.

"I'm pissed at you, too."

"That's not helpful."

"She said she was heading to the Orchid," Kristen said. "Hey, isn't that where you were supposed to meet her to-night?" Kristen added, sarcastically. She could never resist a jab, he thought. "Why'd you blow her off?"

"No reason."

"Quit evading the question, Andy," Kristen said sternly.

"I had a panic attack," Andrew said. Kristen was silent for once. No jabs. No cursing. Just silence on the other end. "What? No barbs?" Andrew asked.

"No barbs," Kristen said. Her tone was subdued. "Go find Olivia and go home. I'll see you tomorrow."

They ended the call and Andrew sat looking at his phone. It was the second most intimate conversation he'd had with his sister in ages. Maybe time could heal things.

A rock bounced on his hood and rolled off the passenger side fender, leaving dimples and scratches in the sheet metal as it skittered across.

Amanda stood on the porch, sporting a feral grin.

"Goddam it," Andrew shouted. He opened the door and stepped out of the truck, dumping shattered safety glass into the driveway. Looking up at Amanda, he shouted to her, "What the hell?"

"What the hell are you doing in my driveway?" Amanda shouted down to him, hefting another rock into throwing position.

"There was no damn reason for that? Are you going to pay for this window?" Andrew said.

"Fuck your window and fuck you! What are you doing here?" Amanda demanded. "I thought we were over? What? You're new bitch girlfriend throw you out?"

"I don't have time for this," Andrew said, waving a dismissive hand at Amanda. He climbed back into the cab and buckled up. He threw the transmission in reverse and flew out of the driveway into the street, cutting the wheel simultaneously and turning the truck into a traffic lane. Fortunately, no one else was on the road when his truck barreled into the street.

"Wait!" Amanda shouted at him. She ran from the porch and into the street, blocking his path.

Leaning out of the busted window, he shouted at her, "Get out of the way, Amanda!"

"No!" she shouted back at him.

"Get out of the way before I run you down!" Andrew revved the engine ominously, making Amanda cower, but she didn't clear out.

Chapter 15

Andrew gunned the truck and peeled away, swerving around Amanda, leaving her cursing in the street. His head spun at the acceleration, but he quickly regained control of his senses. He smiled at her angry, prancing image in the rearview as he drove away. Amanda was in the past, where she would stay. He tore out the development and headed for downtown Newport.

He needed to find Olivia and fix this in person. He understood she was pissed about getting stood up—she had a right to be. But the stuff with Amanda he didn't get. He hadn't even spoken to Amanda; the bitch smashed his window. Unless, Olivia thought he had gone inside . . . he had been lying down in the cab and she wouldn't have been able to see him passed out if she drove by.

Shit. Olivia thought he had gone in Amanda's house . . . late at night, right after blowing her off . . . and he hadn't answered his phone. He pounded the steering wheel with a clenched fist. He was so stupid sometimes. She thought he had returned to Amanda.

He hadn't. She was the past. But had he? He had subconsciously driven himself to Amanda's home. The only thing that had kept him from going inside was that he had been too stupid drunk to physically get himself out of the truck and into the house.

No. He refused to believe it. He had driven here precisely because he was trashed. He would have never driven there sober. He had merely been following a reflex, like driving automatically to work on a day off when you intended to go somewhere else. He had been on autopilot—not subconsciously pining or needing Amanda.

He blinked several times, trying to still the trees spinning past the truck, and eased up on the gas. That fifth had wrecked him.

Kristen had started this. If she hadn't started flirting with Sid, none of this would have happened. Andrew knew it wasn't really his sister's fault, but he wasn't feeling charitable right now.

He thought about what he needed to say to Olivia to get her to understand what had happened. He was so focused on formulating the words he would use when he saw her, the car that pulled out from the intersection on the left caught him completely by surprise. He jerked the wheel right to avoid a collision and plowed through a chain-link fence flattening it, and vaulting onto the lawn behind it. He narrowly missed a tree, clipping several low-hanging branches. Chunks of sod flew in the air, ripped up by the truck's tires as they tore the lawn. Andrew winced as he smacked his head on the top of the cab. He over-steered, causing the truck to fishtail back and forth. He struck a headstone and then another. The bangs and cracks of metal on granite sounded like explosions. Finally, the truck smashed into a monument too big for even his truck to dislodge from its pedestal. The airbags inflated explosively, filling the cab with white balloons.

Andrew climbed out of the truck. The front end was smashed. The grille and bumper hugged the monument the truck had come to rest against. Steam escaped the hood and coolant leaked freely over the ground. The arms on the angel adorning the monument had been broken off from the force of the blow, making it look like a piece of Greco-Roman sculpture.

If Andrew had been wearing a hat, he definitely would have thrown it on the ground. All he could do now was punch the air and kick his fender, which he did along with letting loose a stream of expletives. Of all the things that could have happened, he really needed a car accident right now. And one that was entirely his fault. If he had been paying attention, he would have avoided this mess.

From a car pulled over at the side of the road, a passerby shouted at him, "Jeez! Are you okay, man? You need an ambulance?"

Andrew waved him off, too frustrated to verbalize a response. Shrugging at Andrew's response, the man drove off.

He pounded the fender again. What would he do now? He knew he couldn't stay here. At least he couldn't stay here and not get arrested. He didn't have any doubt he would blow well over the limit. He rummaged through the cab and fetched the half-empty fifth. Miraculously it hadn't leaked or broken in the crash. He flung it deep into the cemetery.

Curious passers-by continued to slow and gawk at him. A few more even stopped to offer aid. He turned them all down, thanking them and saying he was "All set."

He stepped through the broken down fence and proceeded to hoof it into downtown Newport. He figured he was between a quarter and a half a mile from the Orchid. If he hurried, he might still catch Olivia there and be able to apologize to her.

But would she even accept an apology from a fucked-up, shithead like him? As much as he kept telling himself Amanda was the past, he knew deep down they were inextricably linked through little Tia. He wanted to move forward, wanted desperately to escape this hole of despair in his life, but like a muddy hole, he kept slipping down its sides and back to the bottom. He thought Olivia was the lift he needed to escape the past, but there was no escaping, was there? He would go through the rest of his life wallowing in the loss of his little girl.

Maybe Olivia was better off without him. She could find a man that wasn't malfunctioning, like he was, had been, always would be.

He shook his head trying to free it from the cycle of despair. He wasn't destined to sadness for the rest of his life. He deserved to be happy, and Olivia was the one bright shiny spot in his life in a long time. She didn't bring the judgment or destructive forces that Amanda wielded. He deserved to be happy. He repeated the phrase in his head, trying to make it stick; trying to persuade himself that it was true. They had gone over this in therapy, but it was a difficult feat to trick himself into actually believing. What had Heriberto said? *Happiness was within his reach if decided to be happy.* It wasn't external, but internal. Lots of psychobabble, but hadn't it been helpful?

The last several weeks had been his happiest in the past year. Olivia had freed him to be happy—or rather, he had given himself permission to be happy again with Olivia. His energy had returned and the pointlessness of life had been subsumed in the curves or her body and her non-judgmental, non-materialistic companionship; all she seemed to need was him and only him.

He quickened his pace, determined to make it to the Orchid. He prayed she was still there, but even if she had left, he would get a cab and go to her apartment. If she weren't there he'd track her down wherever she went. She needed to know what she meant to him. She wasn't some sort of rebound fling; He wasn't going to return to Amanda. He would set things right between them. He loved her truly and completely. There wasn't any other way to describe the realization that filled him. He hadn't even felt this way about Amanda. The only reason he had stuck with Amanda so long was a combination of lust and the fact she had gotten pregnant. Eventually, even without the accident, he knew they would have split ways. It's why he could never bring himself to marry her, in the first place.

Reflecting off the trees lining the street and windshields of the cars passing by, Andrew saw the telltale flashing of police lights shining behind him. Glancing back, he saw a patrol car pulled over by the break in the fence where his truck had barreled through.

He walked faster.

* * *

Olivia was so upset, she thought about hurling her phone into the street after talking to Andrew but she knew it would be foolish to take out her anger on her phone when it was Andrew she wanted to hurl into the street.

Her ankle was sore and she knew she needed to move, but she just didn't feel like moving. The night was strangely cool and the wind quiet. Except for the nightlife sporadically belching from and being ingested by the restaurants and bars dotting the street, Olivia felt like an invisible observer on her bench; secluded from . . . or maybe that was excluded from . . . the happiness going on around her. Or was it happiness? Partying, impostering for happiness as everyone blindly ran around drunk, deceiving themselves into thinking they were having a good time only to end up puking their guts out the next morning. It was what she had outgrown with Lauren. She didn't want that life anymore, and Andrew was a refreshing break from her old ways.

Andrew. She shouldn't have let this relationship happen. It was stupid of her. It was especially stupid considering the consequences it exposed her to. Leave it to her to continue to be attracted to unavailable men; whether they were just sailors passing through or ex-patients, she was apparently a sucker for them. Was she that damaged? What was wrong with her?

She ran her hands through her hair, circling them around her neck to cradle her face. Her head throbbed. She rubbed her temples with her fingers. Was she getting a migraine? She never got migraines. She sighed, as if the exhale would somehow expel the tumult in her head and guts, but forcing oneself to relax was an oxymoron. She looked back up at the bright stars that still managed to shine through the city lights. She knew there were multitudes more obscured by the halo of light emanating from the streetlights, bars and lit signs, but until you left the city and actually saw, you never knew what you were missing.

Olivia knew what they looked like. She had seen the stars many times out in the dark woods of Foster, far from Newport. Maybe it was time to leave the city; a reboot. She could go somewhere where she could see the stars again. Maybe get a job in a pediatrician's office or something, far away from here. She didn't relish the idea of taking a pay cut—she had student loans to pay off—but maybe it was time to move and take her chances. She didn't even have to stay in Rhode Island; luckily Lauren had talked her into taking her Massachusetts boards, too. She could look for something there too. Blue Cross was always hiring claims adjusters . . . for the first time, anything far away from Newport was looking good. And to think, a few months ago she never would have thought about leaving here. It had been so much fun then, or so she had lied to herself.

Part of her knew she was being reactionary. She had wanted to fall in love with Andrew, wanted him to love her. Relationships had burps, she told herself, why was this any different?

Because he was at his ex's place, a little voice in her head niggled at her.

"Hey," Andrew said. Olivia looked up. Andrew was standing before her. He looked a little disheveled and out of breath, but he was here. "Can I join you?"

Olivia thought about telling him to piss off, but held her tongue. Instead she motioned to the empty space beside her on the bench. Andrew took it, and Olivia noticed he left some space between them, which was a wise move on his part. She noticed his knuckles were bloodied

"How'd you find me?" She finally asked.

"Accident," he said, grinning like he had told some inside joke. The grin just made her want to slap him. Her feelings must have shown on her face, because the grin vanished. "I'm sorry I stood you up. I didn't mean to."

"Where were you?" she asked, daring him to lie to her.

He looked away from her and then back at her face and into her eyes. "I thought I was doing better," he said. He rubbed the back of his head with a hand and looked around.

She didn't understand the delay. Couldn't he just spit it out?

"I had a panic attack," he said finally. "I got drunk at the bar and blacked out or passed out. When I came to, I was parked in Amanda's driveway. I don't think she even knew I was there, until I tried to leave. Then she tried to stop me, actually stood in front of my truck. I don't know why I went there. I think it was just a habit."

"Why didn't you come for me?" Olivia asked, but was relieved to hear that Amanda hadn't been consoling him. Tears welled in her eyes. She resisted the urge to wipe them, but if they pooled-up much more, she was going to have to. "I thought you might have . . . tried to hurt yourself again."

"Yeah. Kristen told me that. No, I wouldn't do that again," he said. "I didn't mean to ditch you. I wasn't thinking straight. I just needed to escape. It's hard to explain." Andrew started bouncing his knee.

"You could have come to me. I could have helped. Don't you trust me?" Olivia asked.

Andrew's knee stopped. He brought his hands together and slowly rubbed them. "You're the most important person in my life right now." he reached over and clasped her hand. "I'm sorry."

"Andrew, it's not that you stood me up, it's that you're first instinct was to go to *her*."

"I'm not seeing her anymore. I didn't leave my truck," Andrew said.

"You went there, though."

"You're not being fair now." Andrew looked a bit put-out, making Olivia angry, but before she could lay into him, he cut her off, saying "I'm here now with you. I'm not with Amanda. I'm not ever going back to her. I just wish I could forget Tia sometimes."

The fight drained from Olivia. "Don't ever say that. You don't wish you could forget your daughter." She leaned in close to him and wrapped her arms around his torso. Andrew slid an arm around her and squeezed her into him. Andrew leaned in and gently kissed her on the lips.

"Hey!" a shout came from down the street. Olivia looked up and saw Lauren, Chris and the crew meandering down the street towards them. Lauren was waving a drunken arm at her, then froze in her tracks, nearly causing Chris to sprawl on the ground, as recognition flashed across her face. "The woodcutter? You and the woodcutter? No way," Lauren said, incredulously. "You were at the bar earlier," she said to Andrew, and then to Olivia, "You didn't come there to hang out with *us*, you were there to see *him*, you minx!"

Chapter 16

Olivia, with help from Lauren, went back to her apartment. As much as she wanted to spend the night at Andrew's, she knew she needed time to think and process everything that had happened. Her nerves were frayed from the worry she had gone through and her ankle was sore. Lauren had wanted her to go to the emergency room, but Olivia had declined. What were they going to do for her; wrap it, give her Motrin and tell her to keep it elevated? She could do that herself, thanks. Besides, Pretzel was on duty, and Olivia didn't have any patience left to put up with the inevitable jabs that would be sent her way by the smug bitch. Not everyone could go to medical school; Pretzel didn't have to be a bitch to everyone.

Lauren tried to get Olivia to spill the beans on Andrew, but Olivia resisted stating she was too tired—which was true—but really she just wasn't in the mood to discuss her relationship with Lauren yet. While she'd desperately wanted to confide in Lauren after discovering Andrew's truck in Amanda's driveway, that initial wave of grief and anger had dissolved. Not that everything had been put right after Andrew found her on the bench, but he had at least calmed her down enough that she could see she was being a bit paranoid or possessive; awful qualities she was having trouble wrapping her head around. She was kind of appalled that she had overreacted so badly. No, that wasn't it; she was still trying to gauge whether she actually had overreacted and what her feelings really were. Did she actually love Andrew enough to be so hurt by him? Was that a good or a bad thing? It was all new to her and confusing. She needed more time to process it and determine where they stood.

She hoped Andrew didn't think she was being flighty. She'd never thought of herself that way before. Now that she thought about it, Andrew would probably laugh at her if she had confided that fear to him, considering Kristen's description of Amanda as a demanding bitch. After her own run-in with Amanda, Olivia didn't think she was anywhere in Amanda's league when it came to playing head-games either.

Lauren finally gave up her interrogation attempts and had soon left to go to stay with Chris, leaving Olivia alone for the night. Despite the drama, she actually slept well; no anxiety kept her up, and bad dreams stayed at bay. She woke early and got ready for work; she had the morning shift and needed to be in by seven to relieve the mid shift. Lauren was supposed to work today, too; she hoped she'd slept off her drunk. Olivia wouldn't be surprised if Lauren called in or was late; it'd probably be better than if she came in dragging ass and cranky.

Olivia locked up the apartment and went downstairs to her car, taking care not to rush down the stairs too fast in case her ankle decided to roll on her again. It was still tender, but definitely not a sprain. Justin had driven her car back last night, which had improved her opinion of him. Too bad he had blown any chance with her when they first met—not that he mattered, she had already fallen headlong into Andrew at that point. But she couldn't avoid the little niggling voice in the back of her head that, under other circumstances, she would have hooked up with him, and they and Lauren and Chris would have had a raucous, oversexed three months; until the lieutenants graduated and they started over again as the next class arrived to take their place.

She got to the hospital and checked in, then went to the second floor to relieve the mid shift and start her rounds. Seth was manning the desk. He shook his hair out of his eyes as she approached.

"Hey, O," Seth greeted her. "Lauren?" he asked.

Olivia shrugged. "She might be running late."

Seth gave knowing smile and grabbed his charts. Standing he said, "Okay then, let's get you briefed up."

They completed the handoff procedures and Olivia signed off on the chart accepting responsibility for the patients in the ward. Seth left, leaving Olivia alone. They hadn't contacted the head nurse yet, giving Lauren a bit more time to show up before they called her a no-show. Fortunately, Lauren arrived only twenty minutes late, looking piqued. Her hair was stringy and eyes had a dull glaze.

Olivia smiled wryly at her.

"Shut up," Lauren said. "I've seen you in worse shape."

Olivia didn't say a word, but pressed her lips together, trying to suppress the smile. Lauren growled at her. Olivia brought Lauren up to speed on the shift and the rest of the morning flew by as they busied themselves with their tasks.

Lauren—showing immense restraint, Olivia thought—didn't even ask her about Andrew as they worked. She knew Lauren had had a pretty rough night, but she couldn't imagine she would have forgotten so easily. It wasn't until their lunch break that Lauren finally cornered her. They had grabbed a table together near the back of the cafeteria where the staff usually congregated, away from the visitors, who tended to congregate near the front section.

"So, tell me. What's he like?" Lauren asked as Olivia bit into her tuna fish sandwich. Lauren's demeanor had turned on a dime from walking dead to bursting and giggly. Olivia finished her bite slowly, then started to describe the tender, kind Andrew she had grown to know over the past weeks, including her frustration with his determination to somehow conquer his inner demons on his own, leading to last night's desperate search for him.

Even though her anger and hurt still simmered in her stomach, she knew it would pass; after describing her relationship with Andrew, she knew she was inextricably attached to him now and couldn't imagine life without him. She just wished she could be sure that Andrew wasn't still hung up on Amanda. Had it been true that he really didn't go into her house? It sounded almost too good to be true, and she wondered if he thought she was gullible. As far as she knew, he had never lied to her before. Still, even if it was true that he had driven to Amanda's on autopilot, reflex, or whatever, that seemed even worse. He was subconsciously still enmeshed with his ex.

"Do you think I'm being stupid? Is he in denial and really still in love with Amanda?" Olivia asked.

"He found you last night, didn't he?" Lauren answered. "He may have ended up there, but he came back to you."

"I don't want him going to her in the first place." Olivia twisted her sleeve with a hand. Her sandwich sat with its single bite removed; Olivia's appetite having left once she got ruminating about Andrew.

"He was at the Orchid earlier—I saw him at the bar. I thought I recognized him, but couldn't place him. I kept racking my brain, trying to remember who he was," Lauren said. "Anyway, he slammed three boilermakers, looked like he was going to puke and bolted out of there like a scared rabbit. It was very strange. I guess what I'm saying is, if he said he had a panic attack, I think I believe it. Where you go from there, I don't know."

That made sense to Olivia, but she still didn't like that Andrew's reflex had been to return to Amanda.

"Hey, it's Andrew Medina. He has a shitload of money and he obviously still likes you. You seem to like him still. I know he's kind of fucked-up, but who wouldn't be after losing a kid, right?" Lauren said. "Give him another chance, O."

Olivia was about to respond when someone stepped in front of their table. Looking up, Dr. Heriberto towered over them.

"Can I speak with you in private for moment," Dr. Heriberto asked Olivia in a strained, simmering voice.

Olivia nodded. Collecting her tray she stood and bid farewell to Lauren. They marched out of the cafeteria. Olivia didn't know what had Heriberto so riled-up; she didn't think she had messed up any of her rounds earlier. Heriberto hunted for a free office or room, only pausing when he found a vacant storage closet. He held the door for Olivia, who cautiously walked in. Heriberto stepped in behind her and closed the door.

"I couldn't help but overhear, and I apologize for pulling you off your break and eavesdropping, but I needed to clarify this: are you dating Andrew Medina?" Heriberto said, practically rambling. Olivia's guts twisted. She hadn't realized Lauren and her had been so loud, or that Heriberto was even nearby. She hemmed and hawed a bit, trying to decide whether to lie or not. Apparently, her delay was answer enough for Heriberto who said, "I see." He rubbed the back of his head and looked around the floor before back at Olivia. "You know the policy about dating patients, right?"

"Yes," Olivia said.

"What am I going to do? I can't believe I've been put in this position." Heriberto said, but didn't seem to be talking to Olivia. "When did this happen?" He asked her finally.

Olivia rubbed a spot on the floor with her shoe and didn't say a word.

"When!" Heriberto commanded, when Olivia wasn't being forthcoming.

"That day," Olivia said. "That day he was admitted." Her eyes were tearing up.

"You . . . ," Heriberto said, but his voice died, tied up in apoplectic fit that was threatening to take control of his entire body. Regaining his control, he said to her, "I can't believe you started a relationship with a suicidal patient while he was in our care? The lack of judgment! Do you know the liability that opens us up to? What if that relationship ends badly, which is often the case with you? What if he hurts himself? Did you think about anything other than yourself?" Heriberto's tirade felt like blows against her body. Tears were flowing freely down Olivia's face. Heriberto paced in the storage room, but there wasn't enough room to take three steps, making him twist in circles.

"I'll tell you what. And I'm being charitable here. You will finish your shift and tender your resignation today. If you don't, I will bring this to the administration and they *will* fire you. Furthermore, I will lodge a complaint with the licensing board and they will seize your license." Heriberto finished, his mouth drawn into a thing frown. His nostrils flared, he was breathing so rapidly.

Olivia felt dizzy. The axe had come, just like she feared. How could she have been so stupid to think she would have gotten away with it? Newport was a small town, everyone knew everybody. Sooner or later, the hospital would have found out and she would have paid the price. Worse, Heriberto was absolutely right; she had abused her position of power over a vulnerable patient. What if Andrew had hurt himself? She choked back a sob. All because she had been weak and let herself get carried away with her emotions, with what she wanted.

"Your answer?" Heriberto demanded. He was still standing in front of her. Her mind was whirling as she struggled to grasp that her career in Newport was finished. She would have to leave Aquidneck Island entirely, foregoing work in neighboring Portsmouth or Middletown. Everyone would ask why she left her last job. She couldn't put *because I was doinking a patient* on the application. She wouldn't have any references, either. Heriberto surely wouldn't be giving her one.

Olivia nodded and meekly said, "Yes."

Heriberto gave one last scowl at her, then turned and left the storage room, slamming the door on the way out. Olivia slid to her knees and cried. She had thrown everything away. She fought to regain her composure; she had to finish her shift. She didn't know how she was going to tell Lauren what had happened.

Having collected herself, at least temporarily, she left storage room and returned to her post. Lauren was busy at the nurses' station, looking like she was finally past the worst of her hangover. She took one look at Olivia and her smile fell flat.

"What happened to you?" Lauren asked, coming out from behind the desk.

"I threw it all away," Olivia said, her voice cracking. "Heriberto demanded my resignation."

Lauren looked shocked. "He overheard us didn't he?" Olivia nodded. "Oh, god it's my fault. I shouldn't have asked you about Andrew." Lauren clasped a hand to her open mouth. "I'm so sorry."

"No. It's all my fault. I'm the one that breached. I knew better, yet I did it anyway." Olivia wiped her eyes again.

"He has to change his mind. You've been nothing but great around here. Just give him a chance to cool down," Lauren said.

"No. He's not going to change his mind," Olivia said, resigned to the fact that her tenure at Newport was over.

She and Lauren worked the rest of shift in relative silence broken every once in a while when Lauren would try to offer Olivia some sort of hope. A "what if" followed by some sort course of action Lauren thought would guarantee Heriberto would change his mind. Olivia brushed it all off. Short of blackmail, and even maybe not even then, Heriberto wasn't changing his mind; he was too principled. Besides, Olivia didn't have anything to blackmail him with anyway. No, she was finished at Newport.

Near the end of her shift, she commandeered the computer and typed out her short resignation letter. After printing it, she signed it and placed it on Heriberto's desk. Fortunately, he wasn't there so she didn't have to confront him and his aura of anger and disappointment again.

"Maybe we could . . . ," Lauren started, but stopped with Olivia's raised hand.

"No more. I can't take it," Olivia said. "Just let me go. There's nothing to figure out. If I just leave, I can eventually get another job. If fight it, Heriberto will see me run out of nursing, permanently."

Olivia said it with as much finality as she could. It seemed to work, as Lauren didn't try to make any other suggestions about what they could do to change Heriberto's mind.

The next shift arrived early to relieve them. Olivia gave Seth a big hug, and he looked at her quizzically, oblivious that Olivia wouldn't be coming back. She deliberately kept him in the dark and swore Lauren to secrecy until she was gone; she didn't want to have to explain what had happened to anyone. She said goodbye to Patrick on the way out, and snuck out of the building, feeling like a trespasser.

Chapter 17

Andrew sat in the back of the courtroom, waiting for his name to be called for his arraignment. His lawyer was waiting in the jury box. Although it wasn't until the next morning, it hadn't taken the police long to find him and charge him with leaving the scene of an accident; a fairly easy task considering he'd left his truck in the cemetery. They hadn't charged him with drunk driving, which was a relief. Although he liked to think that possibly the police hadn't because of his family's standing in the community, he suspected the only reason they hadn't was because by the time they found him he was sober.

"State versus Andrew Medina," the bailiff called.

Andrew stood up and approached the bench. The sheriff let him past the railing, and Andrew stood beside his lawyer at the defendant's table.

The city solicitor for Newport read the charges out loud. The judge asked Andrew how he pled. His attorney responded, "Not guilty, your honor."

The judge set bail and they set a date for his trail. Being a spectator to this orderly dispensation of justice was more than a bit surreal for him. The last time he had been a courtroom it was to confront the man that had run down Tia. He remembered wanting to demand they lock him up forever, but after seeing the man and his obvious remorse, Andrew had ended up pleading for leniency. After all, it was an accident and most of the blame belonged to Andrew for not keeping a better eye on Tia; he could have prevented the accident, something he would never be able to forgive himself for.

"I'll talk to Craig," his lawyer said referring to the solicitor. "You're an upstanding citizen and Craig's generally reasonable. I think if you offer to pay for the repairs, he'll reduce the charges to a misdemeanor and request a filing. After a year, if you keep your nose clean, they'll expunge the record. I can see the judge accepting such a plea, too, but he may want your license suspended for a few months. The judge can be a ball-buster sometimes, especially on suspected DUIs, but they don't have any evidence of that."

Andrew nodded at the lawyer's words. "Of course, I'll pay for the damages," he said.

His truck had been impounded, but the solicitor had already taken photos and cleared it for release so Andrew could have it towed to Gallino's for repair as soon as he got out of the courthouse.

The court case, as irritating as it was, was the least of his worries. Olivia hadn't been returning his calls, and it was driving him crazy. They had left things a bit uncertain two nights ago, but he thought he'd managed to repair the damage. Apparently not. Aside from her cell or going to the hospital, he didn't have any idea about how to contact her. He had never gone to her apartment; he thought she was embarrassed by it. She always warned him away from contacting her at work, but she was leaving him little choice. Maybe he should just take the hint and move one. But he didn't want to. Olivia was the woman he wanted more than anything in his life now. She had brought him a level of stability and love he hadn't experienced in his life, and had been critical to his self-healing, these past weeks. Most of all, her love was unconditional and non-judgmental; she accepted him for who he was and hadn't demanded he change. Olivia was a stark contrast to Amanda. He couldn't bear the thought of losing her now.

He took the courthouse steps two at a time down to the sidewalk. Thumbing his phone, he called Kristen.

"Do I need to send bail money?" she answered.

"Funny," he replied. "I need a favor."

"Shoot."

"Call Olivia for me. Tell her I need to talk to her, it's important."

Thankfully, Kristen confirmed without further question or comment. He made his way to his old '72 Chevelle, parked on the street. He hadn't driven the thing in a year, but it had started up just fine. The cherry-red paint was accented with white racing stripes, and "454" in large white letters, donating the engine size, the biggest made for that production model, adorned the fenders, interrupting the pin striping on the sides. Except of the custom paintjob, the car was otherwise original, painstakingly restored by his dad and him, years ago. The black vinyl seats were cracking and splitting at the seams; he would have to have them reupholstered or replaced soon. The monstrous V8 engine let out a roar as he started it, before settling into a throaty rumble in idle. He goosed the accelerator, making the engine rev loudly; the sound never really grew old, even if he could barely hear the radio over it.

Power and control.

He pulled out into the street and drove to meet Gallino at the impound lot. Andrew paid the impound fee and Gallino towed the poor truck away. It was actually amazing the damage to the truck wasn't worse considering what the section of cemetery looked like after he had barreled through it—completely out of control and powerless to drink.

His phone rang.

"Hello, Kristen," he answered.

"I left her a message. She's not answering my calls either," she said. "Sorry, it was the best I could do."

He thanked her and ended the call. Olivia didn't want to see him anymore. Could he blame her? She obviously didn't believe him about Amanda, or maybe she had seen his arrest in the papers. He was just an asshole she was better off without.

He got back in the Chevelle. He wasn't even sure what to do with himself now. He'd taken a leave of absence from work, leaving Kristen in charge while he sorted things out. She was giddy as a clam to be running the show; at least someone was happy. Letting go of control of the business had been difficult, but he realized it was just another crutch he used. He had been hiding behind his work while he let his soul rot in despair. He couldn't mandate he be happy or better or content; only working at it would do—a job he'd been neglecting.

There was really only one place for him to go now—the hospital. He would find her and make her understand he didn't want to be with anyone else; that she completed him and filled in the dark hole that had been left in his heart since Tia had died.

He gunned the Chevelle and tore down the road. When he arrived at Newport General, he bounded from the car and dashed to the main entrance. The fat guard manning the security desk—his nametag read 'Sullivan'—asked how he could help him.

"Yeah, I need to find a nurse. Olivia Bennett," Andrew responded.

"She's not here, anymore," Sullivan said.

"What?" Andrew asked confused.

"She up and resigned two days ago. Haven't seen her since," Sullivan said, looking a bit sad. It didn't surprise Andrew that someone other than him would be upset to see her go.

Andrew couldn't believe it. Olivia loved nursing and Newport; it was completely out of character for her to just up and leave. He didn't have any way to contact her either, unless . . .

"What about her friend, Lauren? Is she around?" Andrew asked.

"Let me check?" Sullivan said. "Who may I say is calling?"

"Sorry. I'm Andrew Medina. I'm . . . I'm . . . ," Andrew wracked his brain for an excuse or a reason that the guard should even humor him, but none was coming to mind.

"Don't blow a gasket," Sullivan said wryly and then picked up his phone. "Hi, this Patrick. Is Lauren on today? Good. Can I speak with her?" A lengthy pause ensued as Sullivan waited for Lauren to pick up the other end of the line. "Hi, Lauren, there's a man down here looking for Olivia. Name is Andrew Medina . . . Okay." Patrick hung up the line and then he said to Andrew, "Take a seat. She'll be down in a minute."

Andrew didn't have to wait long before Lauren arrived in the lobby, her expression grim.

"Where's Olivia? What happened to her?" Andrew asked, not bothering with a greeting.

"She got sacked," Lauren said.

"The guard said she resigned," Andrew said, nodding his head in Sullivan's direction.

"That's what they told everyone. Heriberto found out she was dating you," Lauren said. "He forced her to resign."

"That doesn't make any sense," Andrew said.

"You were a patient. She was nurse. It isn't allowed," Lauren said, her eyes were growing teary. "And it was my fault, because we were talking about you and Heriberto overheard us."

Andrew was stunned. It never occurred to him that Olivia was jeopardizing her career to be with him, but it made sense; he felt stupid now that it hadn't dawned on him earlier that there would be a problem. He thought the prohibition against dating would only apply to doctors and patients, not everyone in the damned building. It explained Olivia's reluctance for him to pick her up at work or hangout with any of her friends. He just thought she was unusually private, but she had been trying to date him on the down-low all this time.

"No, it's my fault," Andrew said. "I wasn't even thinking about rules."

"Don't flatter yourself. She knew what she was doing. No one ropes Olivia into doing something she doesn't want to," Lauren said. "She acted so strange the last weeks. She had everyone fooled. You sent her flowers didn't you?" Andrew nodded. "Thought so. She spun some yarn that Joel at the Orchid did it. I never believed that for a second. I didn't know who she was seeing, but I was angry with the whoever it was for a long time, because he—you—had torn Olivia away from our routine."

Andrew didn't have the slightest idea what Lauren was talking about or why she was making this confessional to him now. He must have looked as confused as he felt, because Lauren continued, explaining.

"We used to date class after class of the Navy guys going through the warfare center. Every three months, a new bunch of guys. More bar-hopping." Lauren said. "All that stopped when she started dating you. I was pretty jealous. Like, *who is this secret guy that has stolen my Olivia*. It was pretty frustrating."

Lauren's story jogged Andrew's memory of that night at the Orchid with the raucous sailors in the back of the bar and later, outside, when Lauren and the crew of sailors came upon them sitting at the bench.

"Where is she now?" Andrew asked, ignoring Lauren's stories. Everybody had a past. Olivia was no different, and he didn't care who she had been with before. "She's not returning my calls."

Lauren bit her lip, obviously contemplating whether she was going to reveal what she knew to Andrew. He concealed his impatience and tried to project an earnest look. Apparently it worked, as she cracked. "She moved out. I think she went back to stay with her mother in Foster," Lauren said.

"Do you know where?" he pressed.

"I can get an address," Lauren said.

Andrew was about to leave, but then a thought occurred to him. "Where's Heriberto? Is he in?" he asked her.

"Yeah, he's on-call in the emergency room," Lauren said.

"Take me to him."

Lauren looked little put out, but did as he asked, leading him to the doctor's station in the emergency services section.

She paused short of leading him directly to Heriberto himself.

"He can't know I brought you here," Lauren said, looking more than a little panicked.

"Not a problem," Andrew said, reassuring her. "Thanks."

Lauren left. Andrew waited until she had disappeared around the corner, then pushed open the door leading to the doctor's station. Heriberto, the man that had saved his life, was perched on stool, paging through a report. Periodically, he would switch to the computer to type a few keys, before returning his attention to the report.

Andrew swallowed, his mouth a bit dry. He stepped through the door and strode directly to Heriberto. The doctor glanced up from his report and did a double-take when he saw Andrew.

"Andrew?" Heriberto said. As if afflicted by some tick, Heriberto started nervously pulling at his tie. "What are you doing here?"

"Hi, doc," Andrew said, presenting his warmest smile under the circumstances that he could muster. "I think you may have made a mistake."

"Concerning?"

"Olivia Bennett," Andrew said.

"I'm not sure this conversation is appropriate." Heriberto said, but the doctor had a terrible poker face. It was plain he was being evasive. When he realized Andrew wasn't going to let him off the hook, he cleared his throat and continued.

"Andrew, I know you may think that you care about her, but it was improper for her to have become involved with you in the first place. We have certain rules and protocols that must be followed for everyone's safety," Heriberto explained. "Ms. Bennett's disregard for those procedures put you and this institution in peril."

"In peril from who? Me? I don't give a damn about your rules. All I know is that you, Olivia and this hospital saved my life. I'll be forever in your debt. But what you consider a breach of ethics or rules or whatever, is garbage. Did you even talk to me before forcing her out? Did you talk to my counselors about how I was doing? You're worried about whether she took advantage of my vulnerability, but *you never talked to me?*"

Heriberto was getting a little green under the gills.

"I'll let you in on a secret, Doc—Olivia wasn't taking advantage of me. *I was taking advantage of her* all this time. I relied on her kindness, her empathy, her companionship. With her help I climbed up from rock-bottom. She's the only person I connected with. Unfortunately, she was my crutch, too. Something I need to rectify.

"You fired an excellent, superior, hardworking, caring nurse in knee-jerk reaction to a stupid rule because you were pissed. I don't blame you. You have your policies, but don't punish her."

Heriberto sighed and said, "I can't undo anything. What's done is done."

"Of course you can. Call her and ask her to come back. It's that simple," Andrew said.

"It's not that simple," Heriberto barked at him, showing some fight for the first time since Andrew confronted him.

"It's only complicated because you're making it contemplated. It's really very easy to hire her back," Andrew said.

"She violated rules and medical ethics. I can't let this go." Heriberto said.

"I'm not saying let it go. Has she ever had a discipline problem before? No, right?" Heriberto nodded his head in agreement. "Has she ever had work performance problems? Late, drunk, fucking up . . . fucking up whatever she does here?"

Heriberto shook his head, but then added, "Until she started dating a patient with mental health issues."

"But that was the first time, right?" Andrew persisted.

"Yes," Heriberto said, tersely.

"So give her a warning and letter of reprimand in her file. It's a first offense. Don't give her the axe over on a first offense. I can guarantee you, Olivia's not ever going to date another patient again."

Chapter 18

Olivia sat on the couch channel surfing. She had already wrapped the roster of five hundred channels three times, but had no intention of giving up yet. Sooner or later she would find something to watch; something to distract her from the reality of starting her career over; something to distract her from thinking about Andrew, provided he would just stop calling her. She'd finally silenced and hidden her phone so she didn't have to hear or see incoming messages, even going so far as to delete his name from her contacts so his name wouldn't blink on the screen every single time.

"Give it up. You're driving me crazy," her mother complained on Olivia's fourth trip round the channel circuit.

They had finished dinner and had settled in for bad television. Olivia hadn't even been home a day, before thinking it was a huge mistake. Her mother was killing her with kindness and she felt like a stranger in the home she grew up in. Her mother had apparently preserved her room circa Olivia at fifteen, stuffies, pink comforters and all. The goddamn Viceroy poster was still hanging on the wall—it was embarrassing that there was existing evidence she crushed on that awful boy band.

"We just watched yours last," Olivia insisted, while she thumbed the channel up button repeatedly. She knew she was being a terrible guest, but found herself regressing to her teens under her mother's gaze.

"We're not going round and round again. If you can't find something, give it up. I'm not watching half a second of every show on the planet for the next hour, while you try to find something you don't want to watch, brooding the whole time."

Olivia stopped the channel flipping, ending up on bass fishing.

"Come on!"

Olivia ignored her mother's complaints and focused on the struggle evolving in front of her as the angler/host with a thick Boston accent, chippered away while trying to reel in the fish struggling at the end of his line. Oh, she wished she were a fish so she could brainlessly swim away from everything.

"I should have never let you come back."

Olivia continued to ignore her mother's jabs. Her mother had really been a doll, when Olivia asked if she could come home. She had lied to her mother, saying she had been laid off, and her mother took her right back in. Olivia had cried the whole time while she packed as many of her meager possessions as would fit into the Miata, leaving everything else for Lauren. She felt bad leaving Lauren with the lease, but she couldn't afford to stay there without a job. Lauren would find a roommate soon enough, there were always people looking to rent a place.

Her mother got up from her chair and crossed into Olivia's view, blocking the television. "Shut that off and talk to me," her mother commanded.

Olivia reluctantly thumbed the television off. Her mother resumed her seat, pivoting her chair to face Olivia. Olivia didn't budge and stayed facing the television; she knew it was cowardly, but couldn't she find the strength to move.

"Hon, everyone hits a bump in the road. God knows your father and I did. He got laid off from the yard," her mother said referring to the Quonset shipyard where her father had been an electrician of some sort working for a defense contractor on Navy boats, until he passed what seemed oh so long ago. Her mother continued talking, saying, "Then when things picked up, they would call him back. The same will happen for you."

"They won't call me back," Olivia said.

"Then you'll find another job. Something will turn up. I know this was your first big job, but people don't stay put anymore. You'll find something else."

But would Olivia ever find *someone* else? That was the question that vexed her now; why she couldn't sleep at night And why she wondered if running back home had been the right thing to do.

"Just because you got laid off doesn't mean you failed," her mother continued.

"But I did fail." A tear rolled down her cheek, making Olivia feel weak. She didn't want to be weak; she wanted to be strong. She certainly didn't want to cry in front of her mother, but she couldn't even control her own body. Her shoulders shook under the effort of trying to hold back the sob trying to bust loose from her.

"Come, now. What makes you say that? You're being too hard on yourself. You're taking this way too seriously, hon. It's just a job."

But Andrew just wasn't any man. And Olivia couldn't get him out of her mind. Just when she thought he was gone, she would imagine him strolling in with his easy smile and a gentle touch on her shoulders before enveloping her in his strong arms. Just the thought of never being held by those arms again made her ache. She wondered if Amanda felt the same way?

Her mother continued to talk at her, causing her head to pound with anxiety.

"I wasn't laid off!" Olivia blurted, trying to force Andrew out of her head again as much as put a halt to her mother's feel-good advice.

"Then . . . what happened?" Her mother had a puzzled look on her face.

"I resigned." Olivia stayed focused on dead screen of the television, unwilling to look at her mother.

"Why, hon? What happened that was so bad?"

"I fell in love with the wrong man." Olivia got up and wiped her eyes. "I'm sorry, I can't talk about this, right now. I'm going to my room."

Olivia bounded the stairs to the second floor and darted into her room. She slammed the door behind her, childish she knew, and collapsed to the floor, leaning against it.

She needed an exorcist. Someone that could cleanse her mind and spirit of all that was Andrew and reset her back to old, carefree Olivia who just wanted to party and fuck strangers.

* * *

Andrew gunned the accelerator as he left the tollbooth at the Newport Bridge. The Chevelle rocketed down the highway through Jamestown. Cops were often hung out on this side of bridge, but Andrew would risk getting pulled over if it meant reaching Olivia that much sooner. Lauren had come through, and he had Olivia's mother's address in Foster, hell and gone from Newport and out in the sticks.

Forty minutes later, Andrew found himself passing through the sparse village center, if one could call it that. He had made good time; it was still light out, but even with the longer summer days, the light was fading fast. He found the turnoff and headed deep into thick woods. The full canopies of the trees darkened the road, letting only glimpses of the setting sun through. The smooth road turned rough, rutted with frost heaves from past winters. The Chevelle jounced over them, causing Andrew to reluctantly ease up on the accelerator. His frustration only grew when he saw his next turn was onto a dirt road, filled with even more ruts. Luckily he didn't have to travel down it long; only a short distance down the road, his destination appeared on his left. He slowed to a stop. Olivia's Miata was parked in the driveway next to an aging Toyota Civic.

It was a white colonial on the smallish side, with a single chimney poking out the center of the steeply sloped roof. The paint was cracked and peeling in places. There was no lawn so-to-speak; the surrounding trees were so close to the house that they blocked most of the sunlight, leaving the yard a mix of pine needles, scrub and bushes. Overgrown lilac bushes flanked the doorway, hemming in the walk even tighter than the width of the front door. Window unit air conditioners poked out several of the windows, humming away.

Andrew pulled in behind Olivia's car and got out. His hands were sweating, and he wiped them several times on his pant legs. He was about to walk to the front door, when he decided to leave his phone in the car. He tossed the phone on the seat, locked the car, wiped his hands on his pants again, and took a deep breath.

This was stupid, he thought.

He strode to the front door and knocked, before he thought of another reason to delay. After two or three seconds, when he didn't get a response, he knocked again.

"Just a minute," a muffled voice came from behind the door. Andrew heard the *clack* of a deadbolt being thrown, and the door opened, revealing a woman with red hair, streaked with greys. Age lines were starting to creep across her pale face. "Oh, my!" She exclaimed, giving Andrew the once over. Andrew couldn't help but grin at her startled reaction. "You must be Andrew," she said. "Come in. I'm Allison, Olivia's mother."

Andrew stepped into the house. "Thank you. I wasn't sure if I'd be welcome."

"She won't like that I let you in, but it's my house. She's hiding in her room." Turning to her right, she led him out of the foyer and into the dining room. A multitude of what appeared to be collector plates were balanced around a picture rail circling the room. Andrew spotted Elvis and Sir Elton among them, smiling down at him. "Are you a doctor?"

"No" Andrew said, confused at her question. "I run the family business, a tree service, out of Newport."

He followed her through the dining room and into the kitchen. To his immediate left, a stairwell led to the second floor.

"Oh." Allison's voice fell. "Are you married?"

"No, I'm single."

"Then why did my daughter run home? No, never mind. It's none of my business," she said, waving her arms at him. "Go up there and drag her back to reality. And if she won't come out, come get me. I have a spare key. Do you want coffee or tea? I can make some. I think I have some scones, too."

"That's okay, but thanks. She didn't tell you anything about me?" Andrew asked, wondering whether he should feel insulted or not.

"No, but I'm just her mom. Why would she tell me anything?" Allison said. "You didn't cheat on her, did you?"

"No," Andrew said, barely able to contain the smirk at her sarcasm. Andrew looked up at the stairs, but stopped. Turning back to Allison, he asked, "Aren't you going to ask me if I love her?"

"You're here," she said, as if that was answer enough. "Now get up there and bring my sunshine back."

"Which door is it?"

"The shut one at the end of the hall, with 'Olivia' written on it in big pink letters."

Andrew bounded up the stairs. Sure enough, there was the door just as Allison had said. He walked down the hall, trying not to sound like an elephant. Although there was a threadbare runner on the floor, the floorboards creaked as he walked across them. He rapped on the door. A crash followed by cursing.

"It's me," he said. "Let me in."

He tried the knob, but it really was locked. He wondered if her really would have to fetch a key form Allison if Olivia refused. He didn't have to wonder long; after a moment, the door opened a crack.

"Go away," she said, not looking at him.

"No, I need to tell you something."

He didn't get a chance to speak; Olivia had opened the door fully and was pushing past him down the hall.

"Ma!" she shouted. "Why'd you let him in here!"

"It's my house!"

"Goddamn it," Olivia muttered.

Her hair was an unkempt red mass, looking like a bolt of lighting had set fire to a tumbleweed. She was dressed in a fitted tank top, struggling to hold her tits, sweats, waistband rolled down, revealing her bellybutton, and socks; she never looked sexier to him than right now.

As if noticing his scrutiny of her, she crossed her arms and pushed past him back into her room. He wanted to grab her and push her against the hallway door and make her understand, but he kept his arms at his sides.

"Can I come in, please?" he asked, his voice sounding husky even to him.

She picked a sweatshirt out of a chair and pulled it on. "Say what you came to say and leave," she said, her voice cracked though. He stepped inside and, aside from all the junk on the floor from her escape from Newport, could have sworn he stepped into a time capsule. Ponies, unicorns, cheesy posters. The pink bed looked overrun with stuffies. It must have shown on his face because Olivia said, "My mother never packed anything away after I went to school."

"I gather."

"Spit it out." she was facing him now, with arms crossed over her chest and a taut expression on her face.

A chill ran up his back and he felt the hairs on his neck stand up. He coughed and tried to will his shoulders to relax. Olivia hadn't budged.

"I love you. Come back with me. I love you. I don't want any other woman in life, but you. Until I met you, I was a zombie. You saved my life for real. Not just in the hospital, but after, too. I couldn't have done it without you. I don't think you know how much you mean to me. I think about you all the time. Leaving work at the end of the day is the best part of my day because I know I get to see you." Andrew took a step closer Olivia. Her eyes were watering up.

"I can't help what happened the other night. It's hard. Some days, I think about Tia and I just lose any motivation to do anything. Other times, I panic. I can't promise I won't do something crazy again. What I can promise is that I'll continue to work on it. I'll continue counseling. For the longest time, I bottled everything up. I thought if I could chain up everything I was feeling, lock it away, I could master it; starve it to death or something. But it didn't work that way. It just made things worse." Andrew stepped closer.

"Come back with me. I need you and I know you need me too. We're meant for each other. You make me feel like a whole man again. I used to wonder what was the point of any of this? I learned with you life's only worth what you make of it. If shit's all you see, that's all you'll have." Andrew had closed the distance between them and was standing in front of her now. "Happiness comes from the people you have in your life. I want to make the rest of my life with you."

"Stop it!" Olivia cried.

Chapter 19

"Kiss me," Olivia said. She reached her arms under his embracing him and pressed her body to him. The heat of her body was like a warm radiator on a subzero day; he couldn't get close enough. He drew her to him, pressing her tightly against him, the swells of her breasts flattening against his chest. Rivulets of tears ran down her face, framing her trembling lips. Leaning in closer to her, he did as she commanded and never felt happier to obey. Her soft lips accepted his eagerly. Tugging gently at his as they delicately explored the contours of their mouths, savoring each moment as if it were the first time they had ever kissed. His tongue darted and teased against hers, as their kissing grew more earnest. Gently intertwining before retreating and then probing again.

She moved from his mouth to his chin and neck, laying a trail of kisses wherever she roamed, eliciting a gasp from him. She stepped back from him, stealing her heat away. He wanted to protest and close the space between them, but she was already tugging his shirt loose from his pants. He pulled the shirt over his head and tossed it away. He reached for her hungrily, but she held a hand out, halting his advance.

"Close my door," she whispered.

Although he was surprised at her aggressiveness with her mother just downstairs, he turned and did as commanded, being careful to shut the door quietly. Yielding so completely to her will never felt so right. When he turned back to face her, she had already removed the sweatshirt. She looked him in the eyes, before slowly pulling her tank top over head, revealing her full round breasts, each bobbing slightly as the cloth pulled over her erect nipples. Unable to resist the urge, he closed the space between them in three strides and seized her. Olivia gasped as he pressed his face to her breasts and took turns gently sucking in each nipple. She relaxed against his grip, and slowly stroking his hair and ran her hands over his shoulders as he continued to ravish each nipple in turn; Olivia emitting little gasps and coos of delight when he hit a particularly sensitive spot.

She reached down and cupped his face. Lifting his chin to her, she began kissing him again. But she didn't linger on his lips long before working her way down his chin, neck and to his chest. She playfully teased at his nipples with her tongue as she eyed him. She didn't stay long; sinking down lower, she ran her tongue along his stomach working lower and lower. She tugged at his belt, pulling the end free from the buckle, then settled down on her knees and pulled the snap free on his jeans. She ran her hand over the contours of his erection that was already straining at the stiff material. The sensations traveled up his spine, making him moan.

She smiled up at him as she continued to explore him through his pants. He wanted to throw her on the bed and take her now, and urge he restrained because he knew she wouldn't want him to. She was thoroughly enjoying the slow methodical, stimulation. He wondered if she was trying to drive him crazy with her teasing. She hadn't even freed him from his pants and he thought he might lose it any moment.

Olivia unzipped him finally, and tugged at his jeans and boxers enough to pull them over his hips, freeing him. She dragged a finger under his balls, before cupping them in her warm hand. He gasped with delight. She grabbed hold of his shaft with her other hand, but merely held him as if taunting him. She smiled at him as she continued to toy with his balls—she *was* teasing him, gently fondling and stroking each nut until he wanted to beg her to get on with it. But she was in charge now, something he willingly, gladly surrendered to. He smiled back at her, making her own grin widen.

She took him into her mouth and he thought he might explode then and there. The warm, wet sensations sent shivers to his knees, making them buckle, and up his back making him gasp. His body was a puppet to her ministrations. She released him and shifted away. He noticed for the first time he was nearly panting and his pulse pounded in his ears. The volcano that had been building in him subsided. She leaned back from him, supporting her back against her mattress. The pink comforter framed her fair skin and shock of red hair. She bit her lip and raked her eyes up his body.

"It's a long night," she said by way of explanation.

He nodded and said, "Now it's your turn."

Alternately stepping on his heels, he pulled out of his shoes and then pushed his pants and boxers off the rest of the way and kicked them all aside. He never let his gaze waver from Olivia, who continued to watch him from her knees. He reached out a hand to her, which she reached out and clasped. Hauling her to her feet, he kissed her before he sank to his own knees, dragging his fingers and lips down her torso all the way to her navel. Her breaths grew shorter and sharper the lower on her body he traveled. He slipped his thumbs in her waistband and pulled her sweats and panties down her long legs to her ankles. She stepped out of the sweats and panties gingerly, bracing herself on his shoulder, her nails pricking his skin.

After she straightened, he put his hands on her hips and exhaled a warm breath between her thighs. She shivered and made a soft cooing sound.

"Sit back, relax," he said. "I'm going to be down here a while."

"Are you?" she asked coyly, as she sat down onto her pink comforter.

"Most definitely. I'm never letting you go again."

"Promise?"

"Forever." And deep in his heart he knew he meant it. He would bind himself to her; they would be inseparable.

He reached under her knees and lifted, tipping her back until she lost her balance. She pinwheeled her arms and squealed as she fell backwards into the pile of stuffies. Giggling, she swept an armful of stuffies to her and gave them a squeeze. He lifted her legs at the knees and she eagerly retracted them up, spreading her knees apart and exposing her pussy to him. With his right hand he stroked the inner thigh of her left leg before dragging his fingertips across her clit and to her right inner thigh. He stroked her right thigh and dragged his hand back, teasing her again with his fingertips. She sighed and cooed at his touch.

Starting at the inside of her right knee, he laid a trail of kisses up her inner thigh and across to inside of her left knee, pausing a moment to lay several kisses around her pussy and letting his tongue play on her clit. Olivia moaned softly and crushed the stuffies against her body. Leaning in, he ceased teasing her and lapped gently at her clit. He ran his hands up her abdomen, over her ribs, under the stuffies she clung against her, and cupped her breasts as he continued twirling her clit with his tongue and lips, slowly alternating between gentle sucks with his lips and probing with the tip of his tongue. Her stomach trembled and her legs quivered as her breaths grew short and sharp.

"Oh," she said.

Without slowing or changing the attention he was lavishing her clit, he brought his right hand down and probed her opening with a finger.

* * *

Olivia gasped. "Andrew!" she cried as his finger slid over her g-spot, again and again. Her clit was swelling with pleasure and the steady stroking from the inside had caused everything below her hips to tingle. She couldn't hold her legs still anymore; they trembled uncontrollably. Ordinarily she might have felt self-conscious at losing control of body parts, but Andrew had long ago coaxed her into trusting him and her own body; now she couldn't get enough of his attention. He wanted her back, with an intensity that was unnerving. How she would have thought he wanted another, she couldn't fathom.

The ball of pleasure coiled deep inside her, tighter and tighter. She couldn't control her breathing or her voice anymore either, noises escaped her she didn't know she could make. The coil unleashed, sending a spasm through her body, causing her body to clench down on his relentless finger.

"Oh," she cried as the pleasure shot to her toes and her brain, blotting out reason and obliterating any train of thought she had. Aftershocks rippled through her, disorientating her further. The tremors of pleasure slowly subsided, leaving her legs turned to jelly. They flopped to each side as she tried to catch her breath, her sweaty chest heaving as she panted.

Andrew lifted his head. He was smiling, no doubt at the results of his handiwork that had left her feeling like an amorphous blob of pleasure. He climbed up her and kissed her on the mouth, a kiss she vigorously returned. His cock was pressed against her and she knew he ached to be inside her, but she reminded herself that he wasn't in charge anymore.

"On your back," she commanded him. Andrew hesitated as if he were contemplating defying her, but a glare from her stifled whatever he planned and he complied. He rolled to her right as she shifted, making room for him. He pushed himself further up on the mattress, orientating himself lengthwise. His cock stood erect and waiting for her. She crawled over him straddling him. She gripped his cock and tugged, teasing him. She lifted her hips and aligned herself over him, but she didn't settle on him just yet . . . no, she would torment him a little more before letting him enter.

She smiled and he smiled back, but it was a barely-disguised grimace. The corners of his mouth were twitching as if he could barely contain the urge to demand she take him. She rubbed the head of his penis against her pussy, making sure he had a good view as she maneuvered it around her, teasing him further.

He smiled and then chuckled. The tenseness in his shoulders relaxed. Andrew put his arms behind his head and gazed at her. His smile softened and his eyes glistened.

"What? Are you so confident you think I can't make you beg?" she asked.

"Hardly. Jumping in with both feet," he said. "I'm yours, you're mine, and we've got forever. I'm under your control, Olivia, and I'm okay with that."

A warm feeling blossomed in her chest and spread up her neck to her cheeks. Although she thought she was already aroused, his words had stimulated her further, provoking a hunger so fierce in her core she knew that this must be what it was like to love so completely and thoroughly it threatened to consume you.

Not waiting any longer, she drew him into her and settled down, pressing him as deep into as she could. They gasped together as their shared heat flowed seemingly compounded creating a feedback loop that seemed at any moment would turn into a runaway reaction. She ground her hips against his, eliciting another mutual groan from both of them, as she attempted to maneuver him ever deeper inside her.

She placed her hands on his chest to steady herself as she raised her hips and started withdrawing then returning to him, letting his cock slide slowly into and out of her. Her pussy tingled, sending pleasurable sensations rippling up her body.

Andrew brought his arms from behind his head and clasped her hips, gripping her pelvis tightly. His breathing had grown ragged. His eyes never left hers as she continued rising and sinking her hips on him, drawing out the pleasure, but afraid to let it end. She clenched down on him as she raised her hips again, trying to keep him from sliding out of her as she pulled away, only to relax and slide back down onto him. She was so slick with her own pleasure she couldn't hold onto him.

Andrew's body stiffened and he moaned. His eyes shut briefly as his head lolled back. He huffed several short breaths, then his grip on her became like iron. Watching him come sent her over the edge again. Her own orgasm ignited through her body, making her muscles unresponsive as they became paralyzed with overstimulation. She grunted uncontrollably as the pulses of pleasure traveled her body and she thought if it lasted much longer she would pass out from holding her breath.

Slowly the pleasure subsided. Olivia collapsed onto Andrew's chest, and attempted to catch her breath. Andrew's arms enveloped her. She lay there, rising and falling in time with Andrew's breathing, and never wanted to move from there again. Andrew stroked her hair and squeezed her to him.

"Move in with me," Andrew said.

"Yes," she said without hesitation. She looked up at him and saw he was looking at her. "You don't expect me to be a housewife do you?" she asked.

He grinned. "No, but you can if you want."

"I want to be a nurse. I mean I need to be a nurse. I need to do something useful."

He nodded. "I'm supportive of that."

"I'm just not sure I can stay in Newport."

"Why not?" he asked. "Scene getting too dull for you now?" he said, playfully.

"It's just a long commute for wherever I can get a new job."

"You don't need one. You're scheduled to work tomorrow's swing."

"What?"

"You really were ignoring my calls," he muttered. "Didn't Heriberto call you?" he asked.

"I wouldn't know. I haven't been looking at my phone." Olivia replied guiltily. She raised herself to her elbows.

"What did he say? What did you do?"

"When you wouldn't answer or return my calls, I went looking for you at the hospital. I bumped in to Lauren and she explained what had happened. I went to Heriberto and persuaded him to change his mind. He tore up your resignation letter in front of me. You're back on the schedule."

Olivia's mouth fell open. She couldn't believe Heriberto had a change of heart. Her eyes teared-up with joy this time.

"Thank you," she said. Andrew smiled back at her looking smug. "I love you."

"I love you too."

She lunged at his mouth and kissed him fiercely. He returned her kiss with equal intensity.

It was going to be a long night, indeed.

Chapter 20

Olivia tugged at the top of the strapless gown. Her boobs kept threatening to pop out, which she'd known from the beginning was going to be a problem just by looking at the way it had hung on the mannequin, but Lauren had adored the cut and insisted on it. The deal was sealed; there was no way Olivia could turn her down. The boob tape wasn't worth a damn either. Truth, it was a hot dress and it gripped every curve of Olivia's torso, hips and ass, before flowing out around her legs.

Standing beside her in the vestibule of the church, Lauren was twitching and talking and talking and twitching, most of which soared over Olivia's head. She pretended to be listening to Lauren, but had tuned out minutes ago as the speed of Lauren's speech accelerated into hyper-drive. She realized she was being uncharitable—it was Lauren's day— and resolved to refocus her attention on her friend.

It was miraculous they were even standing there. Somehow, Lauren had thrown together an entire wedding in a month—in the summer! And she wasn't even pregnant! Sure, it was a Tuesday, but the feat was remarkable all the same. On such short notice, Olivia probably would have just settled for a justice of the peace. Not Lauren.

Olivia shifted the bouquet she was holding to her other hand and placed a hand on Lauren's bare arm.

"You've never been more beautiful," Olivia said, trying to allay Lauren's fears. "Everything is going to be great, provided Chris doesn't faint when he sees how beautiful you are."

"Who would've thought I'd be getting married?" Lauren said. "And to a lieutenant!" She wiped a tear from her eye. "I always thought you'd get married first."

"Not me, you always got more attention."

"Stop it."

The introduction to the processional march sounded and Lauren froze. "Oh, god, am I ready for this? Tell me I'm ready for this."

"You've never been more ready. Let's go before Chris thinks you ran away."

Lauren's dad opened the doors and kicked the stops in place. "Everybody ready?" he asked. "Oh, my baby! You're so beautiful." He tugged at his tie and fidgeted with his cuffs. Lauren was tearing up again. Lauren's mother came up behind him, followed by Chris's parents.

"Dad!" Lauren's voice cracked.

Olivia teared-up herself. She dabbed her eyes with a hanky she had concealed in her palm, cautious not to mess up her makeup.

"My baby! All grown up and being whisked away from me!" her mother said.

"Mom, you're making me cry again! Chris's first assignment is in Naples, but we'll be back. He promised to keep his eyes peeled for assignments in Newport. But you know . . . needs of the Navy . . . ," Lauren explained, as if she'd been a Navy wife for years now. Olivia couldn't help but smile at her best friend and reformed party girl.

The entrance door opened and Justin stepped inside. "Everything a go?" he asked no one in particular. Lauren's dad gave him the thumbs up and Justin took up his position beside Olivia. Justin was in his dress uniform, which was perfectly tailored for his athletic frame. His blue eyes bored into her as he extended his elbow to her. Olivia put her hand through it. She wasn't worried about him stepping out of line again—and as far as she was concerned, it was all water under the bridge. In some way, if he hadn't gotten his nose bashed in that night, she might not be with Andrew now. The realization made her chuckle. Justin looked at her, his face screwed up disapprovingly, but he didn't ask her what she was laughing about and she didn't elaborate.

Lauren's dad gave the "all ready" sign and the tempo of the music intensified as the organist added flourishes to the processional march. Olivia regained her composure. Glancing back at Justin, she saw his attention was riveted straight ahead again, expressionless.

"Thank you," Olivia said to him.

"What for?" Justin asked. He kept looking straight ahead to the altar where Chris and priest waited.

"For being a jerk that night."

That got his attention. He glanced at her, but resumed looking straight ahead. "Are you kidding me?" he whispered, his tone a bit defensive.

"No, I'm not. It just occurred to me that if you hadn't been a jerk and we hadn't taken a trip to the hospital that night, I might not have fallen in love with Andrew."

"Well, you're welcome . . . I guess," he responded. Olivia stole a glance up at him and saw he was grinning. "I guess you owe me a dance at the reception then," he said. His smile reached his eyes.

"Just one," she agreed. "Lauren will want her photos."

The organist finished his flourishes, finally, and the processional march began.

It was a simple service, there were no ring bearers or flower girls and Olivia and Justin were the only bridesmaid and groomsman. Olivia and Justin led the wedding procession,. followed by Lauren's mom and Chris's parents who left at intervals to be seated. Olivia's stomach burbled; even she was having some butterflies. The right side of the audience was filled with the unfamiliar faces of Chris's family and half a dozen Navies, a few of which Olivia recognized from Chris's circle at the bar. Lauren's family was on the left side along with co-workers from the Hospital; even Pretzel and Heriberto were there. When Olivia had returned to work the next day, Heriberto had merely said "Gad you're back". There was no apology or explanation on either's part, and they both seemed to have silently decided that the whole incident was better left forgotten. Olivia was content with that. Seth waved to her from the back row. She resisted the urge to waive back as she walked down the aisle.

Up near the front, behind Lauren's family, Andrew sat in his grey suit with a green-patterned tie. Olivia's smile brightened when she spotted him. He smiled back and her heart did a little flip. She couldn't wait to be back in his arms again.

At the altar, Chris was pale and his smile was strained. He looked like he could use some Dramamine. Apparently, he was just as nervous as Lauren. Olivia and Justin parted at the head of the aisle. Justin headed to stand by Chris and Olivia took her position at the left where Lauren would stand to take her vows.

The organist began the wedding march. Lauren and her dad marched slowly down the aisle. Lauren's dad's smile couldn't have been bigger and the Lauren's nerves seemingly had a miraculous recovery, because now her chin was held high, smile just so, and she moved gracefully, like a ballerina. Olivia dabbed at her eyes again with her hanky. Stealing a glance at Chris, she saw Chris now stood back straight, shoulders back, with his mouth drawn tight and his eyes focused solely on Lauren.

Olivia looked at Andrew, standing now, in the second row. He wasn't watching the bride like everyone else, but instead looking at her. Her cheeks grew warm and a fire ignited in her belly. Andrew was hers whether or not they ever got married; it was just a mere formality they hadn't gotten around to yet. His charges had been cleared up. He was without a license for ninety days, but he managed. On days her shift allowed, Olivia drove him around; when there were conflicts, Kristen would pick him up. Kristen's relationship with Sid, the guy she had busted Kristen with at the office, had blossomed to the point where they were seeing each other fairly regularly. Andrew and Olivia had even gone out with dinner with them twice since returning to Newport.

Lauren finally arrived at the altar, the wedding march came to close, and the priest requested everyone's attention. The ceremony was brief, uninterrupted and smooth; every bride's wish. Justin hadn't even fumbled with the ring, presenting it on cue and with grace. Lauren was beaming the whole time. Olivia found her own smile was impossible to suppress.

* * *

At the Officers' Club, the DJ kicked the reception off. Lauren and Chris had their first dance. Justin got his dance with Olivia and, surprisingly, was a perfect gentleman. She didn't even have to police any wandering hands and he let her go afterwards.

Then Olivia and Justin then took turns giving their toasts. Lauren looked scared to death Olivia was going to tell an embarrassing story about her—God knew she had plenty to tell. But Olivia resisted the urge to tease her friend and kept it clean. To think, she wasn't going to see her best friend again, possibly for years, brought tears to her eyes, but she couldn't be angry or disappointed, just a strange mix of happy and sad

Olivia barely had a chance to nibble at her chicken croquette before Andrew clasped her hand and led her onto the center of the floor. He turned to face her, stepping in close to her, making her conscious of his presence and the thin fabric of the dress that separated her from his direct touch. She would enjoy letting him peel her out of it later and later couldn't come soon enough.

He placed his other hand at the small of her back and they began the waltz. In her imagination, everyone seemed to disappear and it was just the two of them, alone on the dance floor. She was so riveted on him to the exclusion of everyone else around her, that she had trouble following the music; she followed his rhythm and let it be her guide; stepping when he stepped; twirling when he twirled her.

The past three months swirled through Olivia's head as she struggled to grasp everything that had happened, all the things that had changed in her life to turn everything so thoroughly upside down. The events were too disconnected to blame fate, and it seemed quaint or maudlin to merely fault "falling in love" as the cause. There had to be more certainty, not randomness, in the world.

"What are you thinking?" Andrew asked.

But Olivia didn't have a coherent answer at the tip of her tongue and she hesitated as she tried to collect the words.

Andrew studied her, but she didn't feel pressured or on the spot. He waited for her answer and she let it coalesce, trying not to force it; it was important to not force it. Finally, she gave up trying to find the perfect words. "I guess how crazy everything has been," she said. "But that doesn't express the half of it."

"Things have been crazy," he agreed. "Finding the words is tough. I lived with crazy for so long, I began to think it was normal."

"How do you make sense of it now?" she asked because the question was vexing her. How could she even know if what she was doing was for the right reasons, if she was having so much trouble sorting it all out?

"The simple answer? I don't. I can't." Andrews's eyes grew moist. "But that's not right. I made a choice to live again in this world. I was stuck somewhere else. Somewhere in between living and dying. You helped unstick me." He smiled at her, and she at him. "I'm not sure if that even expresses it right," he added. "But it's all I have."

What he said resonated with her and she began to formulate a cohesive thought about her own metamorphosis, if she could even call it that. They had each been on the precipice of change. Behind them, the past had held them captive. Looking forward, the unknown. Each had feared the future or kept repeating the past, trapped by their demons—Olivia by her ambivalence, inability to commit, and living for the moment as if she'd be twenty-something forever; Andrew unable to move on from his personal tragedy. Not to equate the two, because clearly Andrew had dealt with things she could barely comprehend, but they had both been there, at a crossroads. Only by breaking free and having faith in stepping off into the metaphorical abyss had they found each other.

Was it merely chance? Or was it synergy? They both were undergoing a transformation and their proximity to one another, in time and space, pulled them together. Was that still fate? Olivia didn't believe in fate—and when did she get so metaphysical anyway? Even Lauren had moved into the next phase of her life, which Olivia couldn't be happier for her. Was life just a series of phases you went through, stumbling from one to the next? She pondered it, but didn't have any good answers.

"I guess I was stuck, too. Or maybe a better way to phrase it was I was afraid of doing anything different than the way I always had, even though I knew it wasn't right for me anymore," she said, reminiscing about how stale her partying ways with Lauren had grown.

"That makes two of us. I know why I needed to change; what made you take the risk, though?" He studied her face, waiting for her answer.

"Like you, I wanted to be happy again. Not that I was unhappy, but I wasn't *content* either. I wasn't comfortable in my own skin," she answered.

"And you thought I could make you happy?" He chuckled and gave her another twirl on the dance floor.

Once back in his arms, she looked him in the eye and as sincerely as she could deliver it, said, "Only you—don't ever forget that—*only* you make me happy."

Andrew's gaze at her narrowed and she saw the passion that burned behind them. He leaned in and kissed her on the lips, holding it for what like seemed eternity. She didn't want it to end and he didn't let it. They kissed and danced and kissed; and went over the precipice together.

www.ingramcontent.com/pod-product-compliance
Lightning Source LLC
Chambersburg PA
CBHW030924120626
46554CB00001B/270